MW01106865

With a Name
Like LULU,
Who Needs More Trouble?

With a Name Like LULU, Who Needs More Trouble?

TRICIA SPRINGSTUBB

ILLUSTRATED BY JILL KASTNER

**Delacorte
Press**

Published by
Delacorte Press
Bantam Doubleday Dell Publishing Group, Inc.
666 Fifth Avenue
New York, New York 10103

Text copyright © 1989 by Tricia Springstubb
Illustrations copyright © 1989 by Jill Kastner

Library of Congress Cataloging in Publication Data

Springstubb, Tricia.
    With a name like Lulu, who needs more trouble? / by Tricia Springstubb; illustrated by Jill Kastner.
        p.   cm.
    Summary: Shy and retiring Lulu, whose greatest passion is baseball, finds her life changed dramatically when she saves a toddler who jumps out of an apartment house window.
    ISBN 0-385-29823-4
    [1. Self-confidence—Fiction.   2. Interpersonal relations—Fiction.   3. Mothers and daughters—Fiction.   4. Baseball—Fiction.]   I. Kastner, Jill, ill.   II. Title.
PZ7.S76847Wi   1989
[Fic]—dc19   89-1159
                                                              CIP
                                                               AC
Manufactured in the United States of America

November 1989

10 9 8 7 6 5 4 3 2 1

BG

For my father,
my first hero

Chapter 1

The night before she became a famous hero, Lulu and her parents went to a Chinese restaurant. Lulu's mother, who wore overalls the color of a caution sign and a bandanna over her springy red hair, read aloud from the menu.

" 'General Tso's Chicken'? 'Six Delicacies'? 'Home Style Bean Curd'?" One red curl escaped the bandanna and popped out on her forehead. *Boing!* "How are you ever supposed to decide? I could eat this menu, it all sounds so luscious! Doesn't it, Lulu?"

Lulu tugged on the visor of her baseball cap, then trailed her fingers across her chest—a perfect imitation of the Indians' third-base coach signaling *steal*. Her own brown hair hung down her back in a neat braid, and she wore the same thing she did day in and day out, 365 days a year: blue jeans and a T-shirt. Tonight's read WAHOO! over the Indians' symbol. She raised her menu.

"I hate Chinese food," she said into it.

"What, lambchop?" Her mother leaned across the table. Her big Gypsy earrings swayed, and she smiled so that her crooked front tooth showed. If Lulu had had a tooth like that, she'd never have smiled so wide. But then, she and her mother were not exactly what you'd call two peas in a pod.

She lowered her menu. "I said I'll have a large Pepsi."

"I've got it!" her mother cried. "Kung Pao Chicken! You'll love it! It's got peanuts—your favorite!"

Now Lulu stole a look at her father, who so far hadn't said a word. He was pretending to study his paper placemat, which showed a ferocious fire-breathing dragon. He knew what was coming, all right: The Great Restaurant Massacre, Part 247.

"Peanuts!" repeated Lulu's mother, whose name was Elena. Another curl popped out. "Peanuts! You love them!"

"Not when they're all glopped together with other junk, I don't."

Her mother's smile began to fade. "Oh, no," she said. "Not this again."

"I like *plain* peanuts."

"We're in a Chinese restaurant, not the ball park!"

"You know where I'd rather be! I hate Chinese food."

"You've never even tried it!" cried Elena.

"El," said Lulu's father, whose name was David, "you knew this would happen. It happens every time. Just last week in that Middle Eastern place . . ."

"But that was couscous and falafel! This is chicken and peanuts—things Lulu likes!"

"Not when they're all brown and sticky," said Lulu.

"Not when they're mixed together with all kinds of other stuff and you can't tell what you're getting."

"But, lambchop," said her mother, "being surprised is half the fun!"

"Speak for yourself, Mom."

Elena tore the bandanna off her head, and dark red curls sprang out in every direction—*boing boing boing!* "Lulu Leone Duckworth-Greene!" she cried.

It was a very small restaurant, and people at other tables turned to look at them. Lulu pulled the visor of her cap lower yet and stuck out her lip. At times like this, she wished she chewed tobacco so she'd have a legitimate excuse to spit. It was bad enough having a mother so different from you, you'd once searched the house for adoption papers. And it was bad enough being given the name of a violist your mother had heard play the night before you were born—a name so ridiculous, you planned to officially change it the minute you turned eighteen. You didn't have any choice in your mother or your name. But you'd think, by the time you were ten and a half years old, you'd be allowed to eat what you wanted!

If it had been up to Lulu, she wouldn't have been sitting in this restaurant at all. She'd be at Grammie's kitchen table eating the sloppy Joes (no onions, soft white buns) she'd watched Grammie make this afternoon. But Lulu's mother had insisted on her coming here. She was always trying to get Lulu to try new things. Well, you could drag a kid to bean curd, but you couldn't make her eat.

"If you tried it and didn't like it, that'd be one thing," said Elena. "But not even try? You don't know what you're missing!"

"Who cares what I'm missing? I know what I like."

Her mother leaned even closer. Her eyes flashed. Her red hair bristled. She reminded Lulu of the dragon on the placemat. But before she could speak, the waitress appeared.

"Are you ready to order?"

"Whatever you recommend," said David. "And a large Pepsi, please." He gave the waitress the menus and his everything's-going-to-be-fine-don't-you-worry-for-a-minute smile. It was the smile he used on disgruntled customers in his bike shop.

The waitress brought the Pepsi and three bowls of soup. All sorts of strange, unidentifiable things lurked beneath the steaming surface. Lulu's parents began to eat and agreed it was probably the best hot and sour soup they'd ever had. Hot and sour! Chinese food torture! Lulu took a long drag on her pop. She looked up to find her mother holding out a spoonful.

"Lambchop, remember which way your nose points —forward! Try some!"

"Mom, I'm not really hungry."

Elena set down the spoon. "You have to be hungry. It's after seven, and you're a growing girl who spent all morning at baseball practice and all afternoon helping Grammie in her garden, she told me again she doesn't know what she'd do without you, so I know you're starving, and I swear on my Great Aunt Cordelia's grave, this soup is the best you will ever taste, believe me."

When Elena got upset, she spoke in what Lulu's teacher called run-on sentences. Lulu, who was very good at grammar, never spoke or wrote sentences like that.

"You could try just one taste, Lu," David said. "To make your mother happy," his eyes said.

"No, thank you," said Lulu.

"Here we are! Specialty of the house!" Their waitress set a heaped-up platter in the center of the table. Shrimp, chicken, pork, and a lot of slimy-looking vegetables were all shredded up and tossed together. "Enjoy, enjoy!" urged the waitress, and hurried away.

David filled all their plates. He talked about the good day he'd had at the shop, about the new aluminum racer he'd just gotten in, and about how great the food looked. His warm voice rolled over them all like the smell of the honey whole wheat bread he baked twice a week, and Elena began to look calmer. She pretended not to notice when Lulu took only a couple of bites of plain rice, or when Lulu's straw made that sucking sound in the bottom of the glass. She began to talk about the house she was working on.

"I was stripping wallpaper today. There were cabbage roses on top, then eagles, then purple and green stripes. It's just like a treasure hunt."

Elena fixed up people's houses. She could paint, wallpaper, lay tile, unstick doors, tear up rugs, redo floors— almost anything. She had muscles like an Olympic gymnast. She had taught herself to do all of it, and she was never happier than when she was doing something she'd never tried before, like building a brick arch or knocking down a wall. Every teacher Lulu had ever had had asked her to bring in her mother as a living, breathing example of women's liberation. Every teacher, Lulu was sure, secretly wondered how a fiery woman like *that* could have had a daughter like *her.*

"And how'd the Tribe do today?" David asked, turning to Lulu.

"They lost, seventeen to four. But yesterday they didn't score at all."

"Still in last place?"

"Only by two games!"

David smiled at her. "True-blue Lu," he said.

"Don't you ever get tired of rooting for a team that loses all the time?" asked her mother. "Don't you ever feel like switching teams?"

"Switching teams!" Lulu yelped as if her mother had jabbed her with a chopstick. "What do you mean?"

"The Indians are so bad. Everybody makes fun of them. If you ask me, they don't deserve a loyal fan like you."

"Just because they lose doesn't mean you desert them. I can't believe you said that, Mom! I just can't believe it. It just goes to show, you don't know the first thing about baseball."

"That's very true," her mother said, as if it were a compliment.

"Everything all right?" The waitress appeared once more.

"It's great! The best we ever tasted!" David said too heartily. "What's this dish called?"

The waitress beamed. "Happy Family! Just right for you!"

Did she need glasses?

A little while later, the waitress brought them each a fortune cookie.

" 'Your counsel is golden,' " David read.

" 'Look for surprise from unexpected quarter,' " Elena read.

They both turned to Lulu.

" 'Hidden resources are at your command,' " she read. Even though she didn't believe in fortunes, she felt a little let down. "What's that supposed to mean?"

That night Lulu couldn't get to sleep. It wasn't that she was hungry, since when they got home she had made a peanut butter (creamy style) and jelly (grape) sandwich and washed it down with chocolate milk. And it wasn't just the June heat.

Something else was keeping her awake. Something small and hard and round, like the princess with her pea. Only this something was inside Lulu.

By the light from the streetlamp, she traced the crack that ran down the wall by her bed. Elena was planning to stucco the wall to hide the cracks, but Lulu hoped she wouldn't do it soon. The crack was like a mountain with a small lake at its base, and she was used to it.

The stairs creaked. Her parents were coming up to bed.

"Why'd you let me eat so much?" Her father groaned.

Elena didn't answer.

Lulu lay very still. They'd be sure to think she was asleep by now.

"El? What's wrong, babe?"

"I hate getting angry at her like that. I always feel so rotten afterward."

"You can't make her over."

"We took her to the ocean, and she wouldn't go in because she was afraid crabs would bite her toes. It took her forever to learn to ride a two-wheeler, she was so scared of falling down. Why is she so frightened of so many things?"

"She's sensitive."

"Tonight it's just Chinese food, but who knows what it'll be tomorrow? Her friend Zoe wanted her to go away with her to sleep-away camp for a couple of weeks —you should have seen the look on Lulu's face! As if Zoe were inviting her to take a dip in a tank full of piranhas! How could Zoe even imagine she'd sleep with strangers in a strange place for even one night? So now she's missing out on all kinds of new experiences and new friends—and since Zoe's her only friend, she's alone all the time."

"She's got Grammie."

"All they do is putter around that garden and listen to the Indians lose."

"She has Little League too."

"Baseball! Croquet's more exciting."

"If we can just be patient, I have a feeling—no, I'm sure of it—one of these days she's going to surprise us all."

Lulu's parents closed their door. Lulu lay watching the curtains move at her window. The hems were crooked. Elena had made them. The small, hard thing inside her drew itself smaller and harder. She thought again of how the other customers in the restaurant had looked over at her and her mother tonight—Lulu so small and plain, her mother all fire and gleam.

The small, hard thing drew itself smaller and harder yet.

But her mother didn't know everything! Croquet more exciting than baseball? There was no sport on earth—there was nothing anybody'd ever invented anywhere—more perfect than baseball!

Suddenly, Lulu jumped out of bed and rummaged in the pocket of her jeans. Smoothing out the crumpled fortune, she read it again: *Hidden resources are at your command.*

Going to her desk, she took out the tape and snapped off two small pieces. She stuck the fortune up beside her bed, then stepped back to look at it.

It changed things. The crack in the wall didn't look like a mountain anymore. Now it looked more like a sailboat with a little pennant flapping from the mast. That bothered Lulu a little, but she decided to leave it.

"Hidden resources are at my command," she whispered to herself. Then she crawled back into bed and fell fast asleep.

Chapter 2

By the time she got up the next morning, her parents were already gone. On the kitchen table, between a belt sander and a can of Strip-Ez, stood a box of granola. A note was propped against it.

Good morning, Lambchop!!!!!

I looked in and kissed you before I left—you were sleeping the sleep of the just!!!!!

I'm at that workshop on insulation, but it's over by noon, and Dad and I'll both be at your game, wouldn't miss it for anything, give Gram our love. How about we barbecue tonight, *your* favorite for a change?

Love you this←—→much!!!
Mom

P.S. Try this new cereal I got at the co-op.

All those exclamation points. And all those run-on sentences. Lulu shook her head. She put the granola away and got out her Rice Krispies. Carefully carrying her cereal bowl and a glass of orange juice, she went into the living room and turned on the TV.

While she ate, she watched Saturday-morning cartoons. Most of them were pretty boring, but at least they weren't scary like the shows David liked to watch. After a long day at the bike shop, he'd stretch out on the floor and tune in to one of those detective shows where bad guys suddenly lunge out from behind a door or pull a gun in the middle of a perfectly normal-seeming conversation. Shows like that set Lulu's heart knocking so hard, she was surprised her father, sprawled out beside her, didn't hear it. After watching one of those shows, she hated going up to her room alone. She'd push her door open hard to make sure no one was lurking behind it.

Now she switched off the cartoons and went up to get dressed. There was her fortune, taped to the wall. The words seemed strange in the bright morning-light. What could they mean? What hidden resources? For a moment, Lulu wished they meant courage and fortitude so she could be as daring as the TV heroes. Or at least so she wouldn't have to be afraid to come up the stairs alone at night.

But she doubted it. She'd once read a book about people struck by lightning. A farmer in Iowa suddenly found he could speak fluent Japanese. A New York City brain surgeon became a nun. It would take at least one bolt of lightning, and probably two, to turn Lulu into a hero.

But then, pulling on her baseball cap, Lulu had a wonderful idea. Maybe the hidden resources had to do with baseball! She *could* imagine that, since her one and only daydream was to become the next Bert Watson, the Indians' tiny star shortstop.

The word *love* wasn't strong enough for how Lulu felt about baseball. For one thing, you played it in summer, which was Lulu's favorite season. You played it outside, in the hot sun, on the bright green grass, and while you stood out there on the field waiting for something to happen, you breathed in those hot green summer smells. Things usually didn't move too fast in baseball, which was another thing Lulu liked about it. And it wasn't a rough sport like basketball or football, where giants crashed into each other and grabbed the ball from each other. She liked the patient feeling of baseball. Every time you were up, they gave you at least three chances to make good.

Not that baseball wasn't exciting! It was boring, Elena said. But that only went to show, she didn't know the first thing about the game. All you had to do was think of sliding for home, or hitting one out of the park, or pitching a shutout, or a sudden rally in the bottom of the ninth to know why baseball was the perfect sport. It took incredible skill. It took grit and courage. But it was always polite.

She'd never met anyone who loved baseball the way she did. She'd never met anyone who wanted to talk about it as much as she did. All she had was her day-dream.

Lulu's daydream went like this:

A blazing blue afternoon. The stadium packed with a capacity crowd. In the shade of the Indians' dugout, she bowed her head as the loudspeaker boomed out her name: "Lu Greene!" It was the moment the crowd had been waiting for. As Lulu jogged out onto the field, their cheers seemed to shake the stadium to its foundation. *"Lu . . . Lu . . . Lu . . . Lu!"* Her name bounced off the dazzling blue sky and sailed out over Lake Erie. She was Lu Greene, the Golden Glove. Lu Greene, the Singing Bat. Famous for her grace under pressure, she was the savior Cleveland had been waiting for since 1954, the last time they won a pennant. She was their Hero.

In her daydream, Lulu waved her cap to her fans and then turned toward the box where her parents were sitting. She couldn't make out their faces, but she knew they were there. Her father was eating pistachios. Her mother was sitting perfectly still, the cheers washing over her like sheets of rain in an electrical storm.

Lulu never told anyone about this dream. She saw very well that it would make most people smile. For starters, she was the worst one on her Little League team. Though she really wanted to be a pitcher, she was usually stuck out in right field. Coach Angell only let her pitch when the team was way behind or way ahead.

And then there was the matter of being female. But even in her daydreams, Lulu didn't take unreasonable chances. She was ten and a half. That gave her at least ten years to practice. And it also gave the major leagues ten years to change their policy.

What if her fortune meant her daydream might one day come true?

Just the thought made Lulu's hands itch for the leather of her glove and the weight of her bat. Maybe today, finally, she'd really play well. Maybe today her resources would ooze out from wherever they'd been hiding.

Her game wasn't until three o'clock, a long way off. Thank goodness she had Grammie to visit till then.

Chapter 3

When Lulu came in, Grammie was drinking her coffee and reading her paper, as usual. She passed the sports and comics across the kitchen table. Grammie wasn't much of a talker, which was all right with Lulu. There was a tray of sticky buns, fresh from the oven, and the usual easy-listening station on the radio. As Grammie turned the pages of the Pick 'n' Pay ad, she propped her feet on Edward, her very old, hassock-shaped dog. Edward gave a comfortable groan and went on licking the butter off his morning toast. Grammie had lived in this house for forty years, ever since the day she got married, and she said the only way she'd ever leave it was the same way her husband Wilbert—God rest his soul—had: feet first.

After a while she changed from her duster into her gardening clothes. She gripped the railing and took the back steps very carefully. That winter, on her way out to feed the birds, she'd slipped on the steps and broken her wrist. Now Elena worried about her all the time. She wanted Grammie to rent out one of the extra bedrooms so she wouldn't be alone. Whenever she said that, Grammie sniffed.

"Alone?" she'd say. "Who's alone? Rain or shine, I've got Dependable Dan looking in on me." She meant Lulu.

Now they set out the tomato, pepper, and marigold plants they'd bought for half price yesterday. Grammie fretted that she was planting things so late this year.

"Getting old," she sighed. "But it beats the alternative."

Afterward, as they ate up the leftover sloppy Joes, Lulu considered telling Grammie about her fortune. But then she felt superstitious. What if fortunes were like wishes on birthday candles—if you told, they didn't come true?

At two, Grammie switched from easy listening to the game, and they listened to a couple of innings together.

Lulu fed Edward the soggy leftover buns, while Grammie worked on one of her crocheted pillows. Lulu loved the way Grammie kept the radio turned up loud so you could catch every quiver of excitement or disappointment in the announcer's voice. Lulu had listened to so many Indians games that his voice was as familiar to her as anybody's in her family. Whenever there was a tense situation for the Indians, he clipped off his words in a way that made Lulu's scalp prickle.

He did it now as, with two out and runners on first and second, Willie Upshaw went 3 and 2. A foul tip. Another.

"Break-ing ball," said the announcer, mincing his syllables—and then that wonderful crack of wood on leather had Lulu leaping up from the floor and Grammie dropping her crochet hook. Suddenly, the announcer's words flowed like song.

"A long drive to left . . . Roberts is going back, back . . . can't make the catch! That ball is gone, and Cleveland takes the lead, one to nothing."

Lulu sank back down onto the cool linoleum. She knew that feeling, when the bat connected and instead of a dumb dribble or a crummy little pop-up, you knew you had the real thing—a solid hit. It didn't happen to Lulu very often. But when it did, when her hands didn't sting, that ball went for a ride!

"I say we're contenders this year," Grammie said as Lulu handed her her crochet hook. "What do you say?"

"Oh, yeah," said Lulu, "we're contenders all right."

By the time she left for her game, the Indians were

up by 5 to 2 and cruising. This year they were going to rally, she could tell. The season was young. There was no saying what could happen.

As she jumped on her bike, that expectant feeling tingled in her hands again. You didn't give up on a team because they lost a few. No way. The sky was a bright enamel blue, and the air seemed electric. You didn't give up.

Hidden resources, here I come, she thought, and pedaled hard.

Chapter 4

Lulu passed the Dairy Dell and started downhill. It was a long, gentle hill, and everyone always rode it no-handed. Even Lulu rode it no-handed—in her dreams. In reality, she always chickened out. What if a car suddenly pulled out of the Dairy Dell lot, or there was a rock or a broken bottle she didn't spot till too late? You could get really hurt. Even today, when her hands were tingling, she clutched her handgrips hard.

At the bottom of the hill, she turned left and started

through a section of apartments that always reminded her of the buildings she used to make with her Legos. They were squat and square, as if giant hands had squished them together. They were built so close to the sidewalk that as Lulu rode by, she could look straight into the first-floor windows. She saw blinds hanging crooked, plastic flowers in empty wine bottles, and a TV flickering. Not that she was actually seeing any of it. Instead, she was seeing herself stepping up to the plate. The pitch was a hard little inside slider that forgot to sink, and the instant she swung, she knew it had her name on it. Grinning, she lifted her eyes to watch the ball head for deep center. . . .

What she saw made her heart lurch and her brakes screech.

There in the third-floor window of one of the apartments stood a very little girl. She was so little, she almost looked like one of those talking dolls all the girls in Lulu's class had wanted last Christmas. For a split second, Lulu's panicky brain tried to tell her it *was* a doll. *Ride on!* her brain directed. *You can't really be seeing what you think you're seeing!*

But somehow Lulu was already letting her bike crash to the sidewalk and standing beneath the window. Cupping her hands over her mouth, she yelled, "Hey! Little girl! Cut that out!"

Because the little girl was pushing against the screen. Her face screwed up with concentration, she had flattened both palms against it and was pushing.

"Hey! Stop that! Are you crazy? I said stop it!"

It was an old screen, already pot-bellied, and Lulu thought she could see it fraying around the edges.

"I said stop it! You're going to fall! Are you crazy or something?"

Now the little girl pressed her face against the screen, trying to see where the voice was coming from. She wore a pink sunsuit, and her hair was in two bunchy little pigtails. Her nose squished to a round button as she peered down at Lulu.

"Where's your mother? Go get your mother—you hear me?"

The girl smiled. She called down something that sounded like "Datsun!" Then, like a pink moth, she threw her whole body against the screen.

"No! Stop it! Cut it out!"

The little girl smiled again. "Datsun!" she called. "Datsun!" And *thud* went her body against the dilapidated screen.

Lulu couldn't believe it. She looked up and down the sidewalk, but not another person was in sight. There weren't even any cars passing. Where were grown-ups when you needed them? Where were this baby's parents?

And why is this happening to me?

Thud! Thud!

"Listen to me!" Lulu yelled up. "You stay right there. Don't move! I'm coming up! I'm going to find your mother! *Stop that right now!*"

— 20 —

The little girl started to kick the screen. And then one corner tore out of the frame.

It really was going to happen.

Three stories. A concrete sidewalk. So little and pink!

You're a rotten catch, you'll miss, you'll drop her, she'll get smashed, don't even try, it's none of your business, it's not your fault, maybe someone else will come . . .

The little girl crouched down and put her face out the window. Her tiny fingers furled around the window ledge. Her curls glinted in the sun. Smiling, she raised one hand and waved to Lulu.

But things like this don't happen to me!

She was flying, both arms out like wings. Lulu saw the excited smile on her face. She felt her own stomach drop clean into her sneakers. And then everything went black.

Chapter 5

"Datsun!"

Lulu opened her eyes and looked down into the small, upturned face. The baby wasn't smashed. She didn't even look dented. She was smiling as if she'd gotten exactly what she was after.

And she's in my arms.

"I caught you," said Lulu.

"Caught you," the little girl repeated softly. Then she reached up and pulled Lulu's hair.

Somehow, Lulu was down on both knees. Had she knelt to pray the baby wouldn't jump, or had the impact forced her down? Her knees hurt, that was for sure. But that was all. It was no worse, really, than if she'd stumbled on the sidewalk or fallen racing for a line drive.

"We better get you back to your parents," she said to the little girl, and she couldn't believe how wonderfully normal her own voice sounded. *Normal,* she thought happily. *Everything's going to be back to normal in just a few minutes.* The baby grabbed a fold of her T-shirt and began to suck on it.

Lulu carried her into the foyer of the apartment house. The plate-glass door leading to the stairway was locked. There was a column of buzzers and names next to the mailbox.

"What's your name?" she asked the little girl.

"Name."

Lulu decided to press the button marked SUPER.

The speaker crackled.

"Who's there?" barked a voice.

The baby laughed at the sound.

Lulu said, "I . . . umm . . . I have a little lost girl." *I sound like the announcer in K-mart,* she thought, and

if her heart hadn't still been knocking so hard, she might have laughed too.

A door to the right of the stairs flew open. A red-faced woman wearing a duster just like one of Grammie's shoved open the plate-glass door.

"What in the world?" she demanded, and snatched the baby from Lulu's arms. The baby immediately began to howl.

"Where did you find the poor little thing?" bellowed the woman over the racket. She jiggled the baby on her hip, and the baby cried louder. "Hush now, Jenny, you're all right, you're safe now. Mrs. Wysocki's got you. Where did you find her, I said!"

"Out there."

"On the sidewalk?"

"Well, not exactly. She—"

"I always said this was going to happen. Ask anybody —I always said this would happen one day!" Mrs. Wysocki jiggled the baby harder. She wore stockings that came to her knees, pink bunny slippers, and earrings shaped like slices of watermelon. The earrings spun as she jiggled. "Not two years old, and wandering alone outside! It's just like you read about in the papers! Hush, Jenny, hush!"

"She wasn't wandering alone outside," said Lulu. The woman smelled like Ajax. Lulu didn't understand why she was so angry instead of happy, or what more that crazy baby wanted from her. Jenny was trying to fling herself out of Mrs. Wysocki's arms and back into hers. Lulu decided this would be a good time to hit the road.

But just then, Jenny finally managed to jump out of Mrs. Wysocki's arms. Lulu didn't have any choice but to catch her. Again. The baby stopped crying immediately.

"What do you mean, she wasn't wandering outside? You just said she was!"

"She jumped out the window," said Lulu. "I caught her. That's all."

Jenny removed Lulu's baseball cap and put it in her mouth. Mrs. Wysocki staggered backward.

"Fell out the window! *Fell out the window!* God in heaven!"

It was then that Lulu had her first inkling of what she'd done.

"Fell out the window? And you caught her?" Mrs. Wysocki's watermelon earrings spun like pinwheels. Her red face flushed alarmingly. Suddenly, Lulu realized things weren't going to get back to normal as quickly as she'd hoped. She tried to hand Jenny back to Mrs. Wysocki, but the baby clung with the strength of two chimpanzees.

"Who are you?" Mrs. Wysocki demanded. "What's your name, young lady?"

"Lulu Leone Duckworth-Greene."

She grabbed Lulu's elbow. "You're coming with me."

Bunny slippers slapping her heels, she dragged Lulu up the stairs beside her. Her Ajax smell got stronger, and Lulu realized that her knees really hurt. Where was she? Was this really happening? At the landing she tried to break loose and run back down, but Mrs. Wysocki had a grip like a recess monitor. They climbed another story, Mrs. Wysocki puffing and panting and Jenny, still in Lulu's arms, chewing her cap and covering it with slimy drool. Where was she taking her?

"Here we are," Mrs. Wysocki said with a pant, and rapped on a door marked 3-E. It flew open immediately.

"Mama!" Jenny did her bird imitation one more time as she flew out of Lulu's arms and onto the pale giant of a girl who stood there. The girl caught her automatically, as if she were used to doing it. She looked at Mrs. Wysocki's blustery red face.

"Wh—" she said.

"*Wh* is right," said Mrs. Wysocki. "Tilda, meet Lulu Leone Duckworth-Greene. She just saved your baby's life."

"Oh!" The girl seemed to stop breathing. She turned even paler. She was the tallest female Lulu had ever seen. "Oh!" she gasped. Lulu was afraid Tilda was going to faint. It would be like a tree falling. She wanted to run in and get her a chair.

"*Oh* is right. How many times do I have to tell you, you can't turn your back on a baby this age? Especially a little devil like Jenny. I know you think I'm just a meddling old snoop, but listen to this, Tilda Hubbard. While you were just now doing whatever you figure's more important than watching your baby"—Mrs. Wysocki drew a breath—"she fell out the window!"

"Winnow!" said Jenny proudly.

"Oh!" Jenny's mother groaned and clutched her to

— 26 —

her chest. As Lulu watched, her face seemed to blur, as if a big wet eraser had just rubbed across it.

"Lulu here caught her. If it wasn't for her— Let's not even think about it!"

The girl turned her blurred face toward Lulu. Then she took a step back and slammed the door.

The sound seemed to echo up and down the dingy hall. Lulu's banged-up knees trembled.

Now's your chance! Run for it!

But before she could move, Mrs. Wysocki landed a hand like a catcher's mitt on her shoulder. She shook her head and set the watermelons spinning again.

"Last week that baby came running downstairs naked as a jaybird. If I hadn't been out sweeping, she might've kept right on going out the door and down the street. She's got a streak in her, I'll tell you! But when I brought her back upstairs, do you think Tilda so much as said thank you? Fat chance! She grabbed the baby and slammed the door so hard, it rattled my dentures!

"But this takes the cake! How can she treat you like that? She ought to go down on her knees and kiss your feet."

"I don't want anyone kissing my feet."

"You ought to get a medal." Mrs. Wysocki gave her shoulder a shake. "Stand up straight, dear! You're a hero!"

"Who, me?"

At that moment the door marked 3-E opened again. A long white arm shot out and grabbed Lulu's other shoulder. For a moment, she was afraid she'd split down the middle like a zipper—but then Mrs. Wysocki let go, and Lulu was inside 3-E. The door slammed one more time, this time behind her.

Chapter 6

Tilda zapped a bolt and fastened three locks on the door, then threw her arm back around the baby. Jenny bucked like a baby bronco, but it was no contest. Tilda had a giant's strength.

Behind them, toys lay all over the floor. The only furniture was a broken-down couch and a coffee table. Lulu thought she heard the Indians game, but she knew she must be hallucinating.

Knock knock!

"Tilda! Lulu Leone!" Mrs. Wysocki's voice boomed through the door. "Where's your manners? Where were you raised? Open up!"

"Up!" said Jenny.

Tilda didn't move or speak.

Knock knock knock!

"Tilda Hubbard! Lulu Leone Duckworth-Greene!"

Mrs. Wysocki's voice was so powerful, even Jenny stopped her squirming and looked expectantly from her mother to Lulu. But still Tilda stood like a statue.

"Um, excuse me, but, um . . ." Lulu fumbled for words. Tilda stared at her so that Lulu began to wonder if she *could* talk. "Um, if you don't mind, I have to get going. I was just passing by, you know, and—"

"What? What's that you say, Lulu?" Mrs. Wysocki's voice cannonballed through the thin door. "Lulu?"

"So, it was nice to meet you and your baby, and good-bye for now."

Lulu put her hand on the doorknob, but Tilda lurched forward. That was when Lulu's heart took its second tumble of the day. Looking into Tilda's gray eyes, she knew she'd never in her life seen anyone more scared.

"You have to help me," Tilda whispered.

"Me," whispered Jenny.

"Lulu? Are you all right? What's going on? Remember, you're a hero! Bust yourself right out of there!"

Tilda closed an icy hand over Lulu's. Lulu had to tilt her head way back to look into her face.

"If you're a hero," Tilda whispered, "help me!"

"Hero? Me?"

"Lulu Leone!"

"Help me!"

"Me!" Jenny whispered, and giggled.

"I can't stand out here one more second, you hear me? My blood pressure's already at the boiling point!

One more second, and I'll keel over for sure! You want that on your conscience?"

"Help me!"

"But—"

"All right, then! Nobody can ever say I didn't try! Nobody can say I just stood by and did nothing to help that poor little baby!"

Standing next to the thin door, Tilda and Lulu heard the slap of Mrs. Wysocki's slippers as she walked away. They heard her pause at the top of the stairs, giving them one more chance to open the door.

"Help me," whispered Tilda.

Mrs. Wysocki gave a loud grunt, and her slippers slapped down the stairs. Then everything was quiet. And once again, Lulu thought she heard the Indians game.

"Datsun!" Jenny yelled, and dove from her mother's arms onto the couch. The couch had only three legs, and when Jenny hit it, the pile of newspapers holding one corner skidded out. The couch thumped to the floor, making Jenny wild with joy. Holding on to the back, she began to bounce up and down as hard as she could.

"You shouldn't let her do that," said Lulu. "She'll wreck the couch." Right away she realized what a dumb thing that was to say, since the couch was already wrecked.

But Tilda didn't seem to hear. She was still staring at the door.

"Good riddance!" she suddenly hissed, and shook her fist. Then she whipped around to face Lulu.

Diamond hearts sparkled in her ears, and her eyelids were ultramarine. Her hightops had to be size eleven, at least. Not only was she the tallest girl Lulu had ever met, but she was also possibly the thinnest. Her shirt and shorts stood out from her body as if little puffs of air were blowing through. Lulu imagined her bones were as sharp as knives. Her hair was as light and fine as a baby's. Her eyes glittered like cut glass.

"Come into the kitchen," she commanded Lulu. Lulu knew then that she'd only imagined Tilda was scared. A girl like her scared other people, not vice versa. A girl like her sent other kids scattering off the sidewalk into the gutter to let her pass. "I'll make us some lemonade."

The kitchen was even tinier than the living room. For the first time, Lulu noticed how hot the apartment was. On the kitchen table, a small fan blew the steamy air around. Next to it were a Cabbage Patch doll with a crayoned face and a radio.

"And so, as we go into the bottom of the ninth, it's the Cleveland Indians five, the New York Yankees . . ."

Click! Tilda snapped the radio off. "Have a seat," she ordered Lulu, then reached a packet of lemonade down from the cupboard. She mixed it up and handed Lulu a tall glass.

It tasted like sugar water with sand thrown in. Lulu, who usually drank only her mother's icy fresh-squeezed lemonade, choked a little, then swallowed politely.

"Thank you," she said, putting the glass as far as possible from her on the table.

"Yoos!" Jenny shinnied up her leg. "Yenny wants yoos!"

"It's *juice,* not *yoos,*" said Tilda, pulling the baby off Lulu's leg. "Say *please!*"

"Datsun! Give Yenny yoos!" The baby threw herself into Lulu's lap. Her fat little arm shot out and clicked the radio back on.

"With Mattingly on second, we're seeing some action in the Tribe bullpen. Doc Watson is . . ."

Click! Tilda shut the game off again. "No, no!" she said sternly, and Jenny began to cry.

"She can have some of mine," Lulu said quickly. "I'm not that thirsty." She held the glass to Jenny's lips, and as the baby gulped it down, she said, "Why does she call me Datsun?"

"What?"

"Datsun. That's what she kept saying when she was up in the window."

Suddenly, Tilda's face got that smeary look again, as if she were trying to blur herself straight into nothingness —just disappear into the faded, grungy wallpaper. She lifted Jenny from Lulu's lap and sat in the other chair.

"Did it really happen? You know, what Wysocki said?"

As Lulu explained, the tears dried on Jenny's cheeks. Nestled in her mother's lap, she smiled as if listening to an especially good story.

"Then I caught her. I didn't know who she belonged to, so . . ."

"She . . . she really fell?"

"Spell?" inquired Jenny.

"No. She jumped."

"Yumped," Jenny agreed, and snuggled against her mother.

"Anyhow, that's how it looked," said Lulu. "Like it wasn't an accident, like she meant to do it. The look on her face was like, 'Oh, boy! I never tried *this* before! I wonder what *this* will be like!' "

"I only left her alone for a minute. Maybe two minutes. No matter what that Wysocki told you, I don't—you know. I don't neglect her." Tilda twisted one of Jenny's pigtails around her finger. "Why does she do this stuff? I never knew babies were so . . . my mother said . . . oh, shoot! Who cares what they say? I really do—you know. I really do love—"

Jenny began to snore. Within seconds, she was snoring nearly as loudly as Grammie in front of *Wheel of Fortune.*

"See what I mean? She just can't do anything halfway."

Tilda stood and carried the baby out of the kitchen. Lulu watched her pick her way over the toys on the living-room floor and into the apartment's only other room. She watched Tilda carefully lower the baby into her crib, then put her own face in her hands.

Lulu's ears began to burn. She looked away. " 'I

kissed you before I left,' " she remembered reading.
" *'Dad and I'll both be at your game.'* "

The game! Lulu jumped up from the table and
rushed into the living room. Tilda pulled the bedroom
door shut and was across the living room in two strides.

"What the matter?" she demanded, swiping at her
eyes. "What do you think you're doing?"

"I've got to go."

"You can't! Not yet! I—I haven't even—you know.
Thanked you yet."

"That's okay."

"Have some more lemonade."

"No, thanks." How could she have forgotten her
game? The game in which her hidden resources were
going to come out of hiding? She had never in her
whole life been late for a game, much less missed one.
"Tell Jenny I said so long."

Lulu took a step toward the door and stumbled over a
school bus full of people with round plastic heads. Like
a bolt of lightning, Tilda's arm zapped out and caught
her before she fell.

"You should teach her to pick up her toys," Lulu said.
"Well, so long."

But Tilda didn't let go. Instead, she pulled Lulu so
close, Lulu found herself staring up at her jawbone. Her
banged-up knees began to tremble again.

"You don't have to teach her to pick up her toys if you
don't want," she said to the jawbone. "It was just a
suggestion. I mean, you're her mother. But, um, could

you please let go of my T-shirt now? I think I'm starting to choke."

"I can't let you go." Tilda lowered her chin. Her gray eyes had turned the color of stainless steel. Her mouth had gone as thin as a knife blade. "I am a desperate person."

For the third time that day, Lulu's heart staggered. Three times, and she was out. Tilda pointed to the couch, and she sank down onto it.

Chapter 7

Why'd I have to come by here just then? Why'd I have to come by here at all? But I always come this way. I've ridden past this building a million times, and I never guessed who lived inside. A crazy baby who thinks she can fly. And her mother. A desperate person.

Tilda brought a chair from the kitchen and sat opposite the couch.

"The first thing you should know is I'm a—you know."

A *you know*? What was a *you know*? A murderer? A

kidnapper? A blackmail victim? A millionaire's disowned daughter? The possibilities were suddenly endless. Lulu, who had never been on a roller coaster in her life, felt as dizzy as if she'd just stepped aboard the Cyclone.

"A thief. I stole money. A lot of it."

Lulu tried to imagine Tilda stepping up to a bank teller, a black gun in her long bony fingers. "This is a—you know. A stickup," she'd say.

"Not from a bank," Tilda said, as if reading her mind. "Worse than that."

Tilda lifted her chin, her long jawbone jutting out. Her skinniness wasn't the fragile kind. It was hard and sinewy. What was worse than robbing a bank?

"I took it from my mother," Tilda said. "I forged a check at her bank. It was the easiest thing I ever did. In a hick town like that, if you lived there all your life, they don't ask any questions. Even if you're like me. I left her thirty-five dollars and thirty-seven cents. Jenny and I walked right out of that bank and onto the bus. Jenny loved the bus ride. We had to change buses three times. I guess they can get me for that too. You know—forgery."

Lulu stared. She saw that Tilda's shirt was missing a button and the lace of one hightop was broken. She hadn't noticed those things before, just the beautiful makeup and the diamond earrings. Had Tilda stolen those too?

"I'm hiding out. Nobody knows where I am."

"Not even your husband?"

Tilda jumped up from her chair. She crossed the room, opened Jenny's door, and peeked in. When she came back to Lulu, she tossed her flyaway hair and lifted her long, sharp chin. The diamonds flashed in her ears.

"My husband's in the navy. He—you know. Shipped out months ago, and he'll be gone for a long time."

"That's too bad."

Tilda tossed her hair again.

"He writes me a long love letter every night. He—you know. He can't sleep until he does. He misses me desperately."

Anyone could see from the way her gray eyes grew stormy and her lip trembled that she felt the same way about him.

"Of course he'd rescue us in a minute if he could. But it's—you know. Impossible."

"But—but why didn't he send you money? Why'd you have to steal it from your mother?"

Tilda lowered her chin, and the look she gave Lulu made her remember the way Tilda had gripped her T-shirt when she tried to leave. They said drowning people had strength like that.

"She deserved it, that's why! Ha! I showed her. Didn't I?" When Lulu didn't answer, she took a step closer. Her eyes blazed. Her earrings shot sparks. "Didn't I?"

Lulu threw her hands up over her face. "Yes!" she yelped. "You did! You showed her, all right!"

"Okay. And don't you forget it."

Suddenly Tilda slumped down beside Lulu on the

couch. Lulu moved one finger to peep at her. Tilda looked exhausted. What was wrong with her? Was she what the kids at school called mental? One thing was sure. Out of a crowd of ten thousand, she was the last person Lulu would choose to be locked in a room with.

How am I ever going to get out of here? Suddenly, the words of Coach Angell came to her. *"Aim for the weak spot."* The best batters in the majors, he'd told Lulu's team, study pitchers and learn their weak spots. Then they look for that pitch and slug it. What was Tilda's weak spot?

Suddenly, Lulu knew: She didn't have a *plan.* She'd stolen the money without thinking ahead. Now she was a fugitive trapped in this tiny hot apartment. Maybe if Lulu could convince her she could help her . . .

Lulu pressed her knees together to stop their trembling. She cleared her throat.

"I think you need a plan," she said.

Tilda turned to look at her. For a moment, it was as if she'd forgotten someone was sitting beside her on the couch. Then she sneered, "A plan?"

"It—it sounds like you didn't have one. Like you didn't think ahead. You were so mad at your mom, you just acted on the spur of the moment."

"It's easy for you to say. You're the big hero."

"Who, me?"

"No, I'm talking to that teddy bear."

"But I'm not a hero! It was all an accident."

"Ha! I don't believe in accidents. I believe in fate. You were meant to be a hero, and I—" Tilda's eyes nar-

— 39 —

rowed to a steely squint that made her look like a crook picking a lock. "My mom would love to see me now. I can just see her. She'd cross her arms on her chest and say, 'What'd I tell you? It's all come home to roost!' "

"Huh?"

"I told you, you wouldn't understand. Your mother probably worships the ground you walk on. A kid like you. Always does the right thing. But *me.*"

Tilda tossed her head, and her hair flew like torn silk. The diamonds glittered in her ears. She was a desperado again. A robber queen.

"Every time I ever messed something up, my mother was right there letting me know. Even when I didn't mess up, she said I did. And when I had Jenny—shoot! Jenny and I had to live with her, because—you know. With my husband gone all the time, and everything. . . . First she'd say Jenny had too many clothes on. Then when I took some off, she'd ask if I wanted her to catch her death. She'd say I was feeding her too much and she was going to be fat, then she'd ask me was I trying to starve her to death. All day, from morning to night. And Jenny had colic at first, and she'd cry all day and all night, and my mother made out like that was my fault too. Eighteen months I put up with it. Then, snap! Jenny and I were on that bus."

"I bet she misses you now. She's probably sorry."

"*My* mother? She'd rather jump out a window than— you know. Admit she made a mistake. Anyway, that's not—you know. The worst part."

With a Name Like Lulu, Who Needs More Trouble?

There was another worst part? It was like a nightmare—a dozen fly balls descending on Lulu at once.

"I'm almost out of money. I never knew how much it costs just to live. My mother used to buy the Pampers and baby food and stuff. . . . I don't have enough for next month's rent. Wysocki will kick me out! She'll report me to somebody! She pretends she wants to help me, but she's just like my mother. She's always trying to tell me what to do with Jenny. She hates me because I don't listen to her. But I didn't come all the way here for somebody else to run my life! I came here for . . . for . . ."

Lulu remembered: *Swing for the weak spot.*

"I'm telling you, you need a plan."

"I know that!"

"I'm very good at plans. My grandmother calls me Dependable Dan."

Tilda looked Lulu up and down. Lulu knew what she was thinking: *She's just a kid. A short, scrawny one at that.* Lulu tried to sit up straighter. She tried to put a gutsy, brave look on her petrified face.

"How old are you?"

"Ten and a half."

"Shoot!"

"I might be able to help you. I've lived in Cleveland all my life. I know my way around, and my parents have a lot of friends. I have a lot of—you know. Resources."

Tilda's eyes narrowed to that steely squint.

"You saved Jenny. Shoot, what have I got to lose?

You've got to swear you won't betray me, though. Remember, I'm hiding out."

"I swear."

"Really?"

"Do you have a Bible?"

"No, but here." Tilda picked up a small fat magazine from beside the couch. *Baseball Digest.* Lulu was too far gone to even wonder about that. She put her right hand over a photo of Roger Clemens.

"I swear," she said.

"Now, write down your phone number, right here. Good." In one stride, Tilda was at the door. She undid the locks and the bolt. "I'll call you tomorrow morning."

Lulu staggered down the stairs and through the front door. She grabbed up her bike from where she'd dropped it on the sidewalk. The strength flowed back into her wobbly legs, and she began to pedal as hard as she could. She didn't dare look back, sure that either Mrs. Wysocki, bunny slippers flapping, or Tilda, bony legs pumping like pistons, would be after her.

At least I had the sense to write down a fake phone number.

As she sped around the corner, Lulu began to work out a new route from Grammie's house to the ball field. Never, ever, ever again would she go anywhere near that terrible place.

Chapter 8

The game had just ended. She'd missed a game for the first time in her life. Lulu's teammates were all gathered around Coach Angell. The parents were folding up their lawn chairs.

How was she going to explain to the coach and her parents where she'd been? She couldn't tell them the truth. Elena would make a huge fuss. She'd want to go straight back to the apartment and meet Tilda and the baby. Even if Lulu told her that was the last place on earth she ever wanted to see, Elena wouldn't care. She'd drag Lulu. That was how she was.

I'll have to make up a story, Lulu thought. *I already told Tilda one—I said I'd be back. When I won't. Not ever. So now I'll have to lie to my mother and my coach too.*

But what could she say? That she'd been caught in a freak thunderstorm and struck by lightning? Everyone knew it would take at least that to keep Lulu from a game. But she wasn't any good at making up lies. Lies were wrong, and besides, she'd never had anything to lie about.

Till now.

Just then, an orange VW bug with a bike rack on top sped into the parking lot and lurched to a stop, missing Coach Angell's new Voyager by inches. The driver's door flew open, and Elena, waving her arms over her head, came running across the grass.

"Here we are, lambchop! I'm so sorry! You won't believe, the whole day's been a disaster! First I lost track of time, then the car overheated right at an intersection, horns blaring, I had to run into this guy's house and beg him for some water, then I remembered I left my good fountain pen, the one Grammie gave me for high school graduation, back at the workshop. Then they're still doing work on the Shoreway, and I had to take this horrendous detour, then right after I picked up Daddy, the car overheated again, smoking like a dragon, didn't it, David?"

Lulu's father had ambled up by now, and he smiled apologetically. "You know we really meant to be here," he said.

"How'd you do?" asked Elena. "Did you get a piece of it?"

Elena knew about three lines of baseball talk, and *get a piece of it* was one of them.

"Well," said Lulu, "not today." She was so relieved, she made a joke. "I did make one good catch, though."

"That's great, Lu. I wish we could've seen it."

"You wouldn't have believed it, Mom. Just a minute. I have to tell the coach something."

They didn't know! She didn't have to make up a lie!

Lulu bounded across the grass. The nightmare was over. She could pretend none of it had ever happened. By tomorrow, her life would be completely back to normal.

"Lulu! I was worried about you!" Coach Angell looked up from his clipboard. His brow wrinkled so that all the freckles squished together. "Are you all right?"

Lulu would never have been able to lie beneath that kindly gaze. "I'm all right now," she said. "But before, I —I just wasn't feeling myself."

"You take it easy then. We won, but only by the skin of our teeth. I'm depending on you next time. I want you to give us your hundred percent, all right?"

"You can depend on me! My grandmother calls me Dependable Dan!"

"All right!" He gave her a pat on the back and waved at her parents. Lulu ran back to them.

"Are you hungry, lambchop? Are you ready for that barbecue I promised?"

"I'm starving, Mom."

"Let's go."

Elena drove with one arm out the window, her hair streaming back like dark red ribbons. Beside her, David sang Beatles songs. Slouched in the backseat, Lulu felt as if she were getting over the flu. Still weak, shaky, and a little dizzy, but with the worst behind her. Tilda, Jenny, Mrs. Wysocki—they were almost like something she had imagined while delirious with fever. Things like that couldn't *really* happen to her. As soon as they got home, she'd go up to her room, close the door, lie down on her bed, and find a recap of the Indians game on the radio. The smell of the barbecue would drift up, and—

"What in the world?" cried Elena. "Who's holding their convention on our front lawn?"

Lulu bolted up. There on the lawn, flanked by people with cameras and tape recorders, was Mrs. Wysocki. As the car swung into the driveway, she lowered her head and barreled toward it.

Chapter 9

"Lulu Leone Duckworth-Greene! Meet your public, dear!" Mrs. Wysocki yanked open the car door and reached for Lulu, but Elena jumped in front of her.

"What do you think you're doing?"

Mrs. Wysocki straightened up. "Who are you?"

"Who am I? I'm her mother! Who are you?"

Mrs. Wysocki had changed her housecoat for a hot pink dress printed with giant peacocks, and her slippers for sandals with little jewels glued to the straps. The watermelons still spun in her ears.

"*You're* her mother? You don't look a thing like her."

"Lulu, do you know this woman?" Elena demanded.

"I . . . uh . . ."

"Well, if you are her mother, I have to hand it to you." Mrs. Wysocki grabbed Elena's hand and pumped it. "This is her mother," she called over her shoulder to the others. "You'll want to interview her too." She turned to Elena and said in a confiding voice, "They'll want your secret formula, dear. How you managed to raise a girl like that, in this day and age, with most of our youth going to rack and ruination."

"Is this the heroine?" A man's face poked in the car window. "Is this little Zulu?"

"*Lulu.* Lulu Leone Duckworth-Greene. And I'm Mary Anne Wysocki. Don't forget the *e* on the *Anne.*"

"A heroine!" cried Elena. "Lulu?"

"Lulu Leone. That's a wild one. How do you spell *Leone*?"

When Lulu was six years old, on the night before the first day of first grade, she had tried to discover a formula for Disappearing Juice. Now, more than ever in her life, she wished that she'd succeeded.

"Lulu Leone Duckworth-Greene. I've got a good memory for names, if I do say so myself, and that one's burned into my brain. I can still hear her saying it, standing there with that poor little lamb Jenny in her arms."

"Little lamb? Lulu, get out of that car!"

Lulu scrunched down even deeper. Eyes squeezed

shut, she saw Tilda trying to blur herself into the living-room wallpaper.

" 'Fell out the window!' I said. 'God in heaven!' I said. Not that I take the name of the Lord in vain every day."

"Who fell out the window? Lulu!"

A large warm hand settled gently on her shoulder. Lulu opened her eyes to see her father, who was still sitting in the front seat.

"Hey. Come on. Nothing we can't handle together, right?"

Lulu inched toward the door. It seemed to take at least two hours to climb out.

Then everything went fast forward. A man and a woman identified themselves as reporters from the *Sun Press* and the *Plain Dealer*. They showed David their press cards and asked Lulu to tell her story.

"In your own words. As well as you can."

Snap! went a camera. Whomp! went Mrs. Wysocki's catcher's mitt of a hand on Lulu's shoulder. One reporter held out a little mike. The other had his ballpoint poised in midair. Sweat stood out on Lulu's brow. Her ears felt charcoal broiled. The sloppy Joes she'd eaten for lunch tried hard to make a repeat performance. Elena looked ready to jump out of her skin.

"Don't be scared!" she urged Lulu. "Just tell us what happened, lambchop! We're dying to hear!"

Didn't she know that was exactly the problem? How could Lulu talk, with four strangers staring at her as if she were the two-headed chicken in the sideshow? A tidal wave of sloppy Joes rose inside her. Her ears burned hotter yet.

The reporter with the midair ball-point frowned at Mrs. Wysocki. He was beginning to wonder if she'd made the whole thing up. Now Elena said in a coaxing voice, "We're all waiting, Lu."

What an understanding mother! everyone thought. *And beautiful too.* Lulu was the only one who heard the hidden message in her mother's words: *What's the matter with you, anyway?*

"Never mind!" boomed Mrs. Wysocki, landing a brain-scrambling pat on Lulu's head. "If she won't blow her own horn, I'll blow it for her!"

And she launched into the story. The reporters and photographers slapped their foreheads. They snorted. They grinned. They hung on her every word. Mrs. Wysocki's earrings spun. Her cheeks were as red as Santa's.

"Incredible!"

"Fantastic!"

"What a story! AP will pick this up, honey! You'll be national news!"

"And afterward she tried to disappear on me," said Mrs. Wysocki. "Have you got my name right? Don't forget the *e* on the *Anne.* For the life of me, I couldn't figure out why she hid in that apartment—with *her*— but then it came to me: Lulu's modest! She acts like she'd just as soon forget the whole thing happened! Doesn't want an ounce of credit. Not that Tilda would give her any anyway."

"Can we have one more with both the parents? Did you say she's ten? She's small for her age, isn't she? What's the baby like? Is she cute?"

"A living doll! Wait till you see her. She'll break your heart!"

"You'll come back with us to Mrs. Wysocki's, won't you, honey?" The reporter with the microphone bent to Lulu. She had a long, sharp nose and small snapping eyes. She smelled like the perfume counter at Higbee's. "That way we can get a shot of you and the baby together. This is a slow day so far. Don't be surprised if you see yourself on the front page tomorrow."

"You can't go there!" Lulu cried.

The reporter straightened, suddenly alert. "Why not? Is something wrong?"

Wrong! Nothing's right! The baby's more like an alien than a living doll, and her mother's a fugitive from justice. A desperate person! If you go there now, there's no telling what will happen.

Lulu stuttered. "She . . . I . . . you . . ."

Once more, Mrs. Wysocki took over. "You can go there, but don't count on her giving you an interview. She's not the friendly type. Lulu's the first person I've seen go into her place, and Tilda's been there a solid month. She treats me like I'm a walking case of the plague."

The reporter looked even more interested. She had eyes like a weasel. "You make it sound as if she's got something to hide."

"She's a strange one, that's for sure."

The reporter leaned down to Lulu. "But she let *you* in, didn't she? And no wonder! She owes you everything, doesn't she? She'd probably do anything for you. Won't you come back with us to the apartment?"

"No!"

"No? Are you sure, honey? It's such a wonderful story. You'll warm the hearts of people all over the country."

"No, I won't! Not when they know the truth!"

The reporter's beady eyes widened. Her nose was as sharp as a can opener.

"The truth? What are you talking about, honeybunch?"

"Nothing! Forget it! Oh!" Lulu's brain suddenly slipped out of gear. She couldn't lie, she couldn't tell the truth. She realized she'd begun to cry.

"That's enough for now," she heard her father say. His arm was around her waist, and he was steering her up the front walk.

"Can I come back in an hour, when she's had a little rest?" The reporter was following them. "Could we arrange—"

"That's enough," David said firmly. He closed the front door, and Lulu and her parents stood in the hallway looking at each other.

"Lambchop," said Elena, "did you really do that? Save that baby?"

Lulu rubbed her eyes. "I guess so," she said.

Her mother took her face in her strong hands. The

tips of her fingers were like sandpaper. Tears stood in her eyes too.

"I'm so proud of you," she said.

Lulu swallowed. "You are?"

"Oh, lambchop." And her mother folded her in her arms.

Chapter 10

Lulu sat at the kitchen table, oiling her glove. On the table before her was the Sunday paper. In the middle of the front page was a photo of a girl in a T-shirt that said WAHOO! A large hand was gripping her shoulder. The girl looked as if she were about to be attacked by grizzlies. The caption read:

> Lulu Leone Duckworth-Greene, 10, became a hero out of the blue yesterday when she caught an 18-month-old baby as it fell from the third-floor window of an apartment. Both Lulu and the baby are fine. Story, p. 1B.

There was another photo on 1B. Mrs. Wysocki was in this one, clasping the girl as if she were a bowling trophy she'd just won. The story was headlined LITTLE LEAGUER MAKES CATCH OF HER CAREER.

"I just put out my arms and she jumped into them, that's all," said Lulu Leone Duckworth-Greene. "It wasn't any big deal."

Little Jennifer Hubbard can't talk very well yet, but if she could she'd undoubtedly disagree. Yesterday, the tiny toddler fell three floors from her apartment window, landing not on the concrete sidewalk but in Lulu's arms.

Lulu, 10, was on her way to . . .

"Ashtabula? Really? That's super of you—thanks a lot —but my daughter's not exactly an extrovert, and . . . Okay, sure. Sure, I'll ask her. What's your number there?"

Across the room, Elena was on the phone, as she had been all morning. She was standing on one leg like a flamingo and wearing a T-shirt that said ELSIE'S GARAGE—WE'RE ALWAYS ON OUR TOWS. Now she wrote something down and turned to Lulu with a grin.

"The principal of an elementary school in Ashtabula," she said. "He wants you to come speak to his students about believing in yourself. He wants to make you an honorary—"

Ring ring!

"Hello? . . . Oh, really? Wow, thanks a lot, but Lulu

doesn't like tacos. . . . No, not burritos or enchiladas either. You don't make sloppy Joes, do you?"

Her grin was even wider this time. She shook her jumbled red curls as she hung up. Lulu could see she was having the time of her life.

"Nacho Grande wants to give you—"

Ring ring!

"Hello?"

Lulu looked back down at the newspaper. *So that really is me,* she thought. Her name didn't seem quite as ridiculous when it had *hero* after it.

Slowly, deliberately, Lulu worked the oil into each seam of her glove. When she'd come downstairs for breakfast this morning, Elena had been at the stove cooking an avocado and tofu omelet.

"It's hero food!" she'd cried happily, sliding it onto a plate and putting it down at Lulu's place. Lulu had stared at the thing in disbelief. Had her mother forgotten that Lulu never ate anything with lumps in it—especially slimy green and rubbery white lumps?

She must have forgotten, because she stood there looking at both Lulu and the omelet with a look so loving that Lulu remembered all over again that hug her mother had given her last night: *"I'm so proud of you."* The words had whispered in Lulu's ear all night long as she slept, the sweetest of dreams. This morning, with her mother smiling at her like that, she took a big bite of the omelet.

The instant it touched her tongue, she came to her senses. The thing tasted as revolting as it looked. Only by a supreme effort did Lulu swallow it, and then she staggered to the refrigerator for a large swig of milk to wash it down. A familiar look flickered across Elena's face—but then the phone had begun ringing, and it had never stopped.

Now it was almost noon, and here Lulu sat with her glove. So far, she hadn't talked to any of the callers. Her mother had tried to get her to come to the phone at first, but Lulu just shook her head. She grabbed her throat.

"I think I'm getting laryngitis," she croaked. That same look had flickered across her mother's face, but she'd been so busy answering the phone, they hadn't had more than a couple of minutes to talk.

"That was Daddy," she said now, hanging up. "He said he's already had three people come in and congratulate him on having such a wonderful daughter."

"Oh," said Lulu. She worked at the glove. Her father was proud of her too. Nobody had believed her when she'd said the rescue had been an accident. She'd done it, hadn't she? She'd run over beneath the window and caught the baby. What was accidental about that?

Lulu didn't know how to explain to them that she hadn't *wanted* to do it. She'd done it somehow in spite of herself.

And now this big fuss was making her very uncomfortable. She felt as if people were giving credit to the wrong person. *She* wasn't a hero. *She* didn't have anything to say to all these people. She was still the same old Lulu, who couldn't make it up to the teacher's desk without tripping, who lay awake half the night before she had to give an oral report, who couldn't dive or ice skate and who always struck out under pressure. Sitting here in her own kitchen, with the phone ringing and her mother beaming, she felt like the world's biggest fake.

And that wasn't all.

The newspaper mentioned Jenny and Tilda's names three times. It gave their address. That was bad news for a desperate fugitive from justice. Tilda was going to get caught.

That should have made Lulu glad. She should have been relieved. But she wasn't. Instead, she was worried. And she didn't know why. How had everything gotten so confused overnight?

Lulu's mother sat down across the table. She tilted her chair back on two legs, a habit that always made Lulu nervous.

"Aren't you done with that glove yet?"

"You have to get every part," Lulu said, and watched Elena tilt back a little farther.

"How do your knees feel now?" she asked.

"A little better."

"I still can't believe all this, lambchop." Elena fixed Lulu with a searching look. Lulu knew what that meant. Her mother wanted her to talk about how she felt. Elena's favorite conversations were the ones where people "opened up" and "spilled their guts." She could never understand that some people would rather keep their guts tidily inside.

"Me either," said Lulu.

"You were so brave. Remember how when you were little you loved that book, *Ramona the Brave*? Now it could be *Lulu the Brave.*"

Lulu worked at the glove. She hadn't loved that book —her mother had. She'd thought Ramona was too pushy and loud and deserved all the trouble she got into. But it was no use telling her mother that.

"And even TV. I know you're still too shook up to talk on the phone, but I hope you'll think about being on that cable show, *Stars of the Heights.*"

Lulu set down her glove. She shook her head.

"No?"

"I don't want to, Mom."

"But why not?"

"Too scary."

"Scary!" Elena brought all four chair legs down with a crash. "Lambchop! People want to praise you! They want to thank you and fuss over you! And you act like they want to stand you in front of a firing squad!"

Before Lulu could answer, the phone rang again.

"You get it this time," Elena said, but Lulu shook her head. Her mother jumped up, turning her back on Lulu, and the small round thing inside her grew as hard as a stone.

"Mrs. Wysocki!"

Lulu sat up straight. Her mother was frowning.

"Move out? That's weird."

Lulu stood up.

"I'll talk to her," she said, and took the phone.

"Lulu!" Mrs. Wysocki's voice roared in Lulu's ear. "We're celebrities, dear!"

"Is something wrong with Tilda?"

"She just came down here and said she's leaving. Today! She wanted her security deposit back, but I told her, 'No way, José! Not if you break your lease.' It's right there in writing—she signed it. She looked like she'd pass out, and then that baby started crying. They could use her for tornado drills! 'What can I do?' I said. 'It's right there in writing! I can't go making exceptions.' "

"Is she still there?"

"Where's she gonna go? She doesn't even have a car. God in heaven! My phone's been ringing all morning with people trying to get in touch with her. She must have hers off the hook. I told that reporter she was a strange fish. How about you, dear? The mayor call yet? If he does, I'll be more than happy to accompany you to city hall."

Lulu hung up. Maybe Tilda wasn't answering her phone because she'd already left town. But where would she go with no car, no money, the law on her tail, and that tornado siren of a baby? It wasn't any of Lulu's business. She'd saved them once—it wasn't up to her to save them all over again, that was for sure. It wasn't any of her business at all.

The phone rang again. Lulu, standing there, answered it before she remembered she wasn't answering the phone today.

"Hello?"

"You told."

"Huh?"

"You swore," came the hiss, "then you ratted. Just had to brag, didn't you? And they call you a hero. Ha! You've got as much honor as a doorknob!"

"But it wasn't me! It was—"

"I trusted you! I must have been blind! Thanks a lot, rat!"

Slam! The phone went down in Lulu's ear.

Of course Tilda had read Lulu's name in the newspaper and looked up her real phone number. That was easy to explain. There was only one Duckworth-Greene in the city. Why hadn't Lulu thought of that?

But never, ever had she thought Tilda would call her a liar. A liar and a bragger.

How could Tilda have such a hundred percent wrong picture of who Lulu was? Just like all these people calling her a hero. Just like Lulu's own mother. Just like that gremlin Jenny, who called her Datsun, as if she weren't seeing Lulu at all but some other person.

Ring ring!

Lulu, in a trance, picked up the receiver again.

"Plus," came the hiss, "you promised to help me make a plan. Don't worry. I don't expect someone like you to keep a promise." Slam!

"You're finally answering the phone!" said Elena. "Hurray! See, it's not so bad, is it? Having people tell you how wonderful you are? You could even get used to it, couldn't you?"

She'd made a promise she never meant to keep. That was bad. That was cheating. It was against all the rules.

Even when you were dealing with a desperado, you ought to be a good sportsman.

"I'm going for a bike ride, Mom."

"What? But the phone! I thought—"

"I need some fresh air."

"Right now?"

"I'll just be gone half an hour."

Ten minutes to get there, ten minutes to explain, ten minutes to get home. Lulu estimated the time exactly, as usual. She'd never meant to go anywhere near that apartment again, but she had to set Tilda straight.

> Number 1: She wasn't a real hero.
> Number 2: She didn't deserve or want any praise.
> Number 3: It was Mrs. Wysocki who'd blabbed.
> Number 4: Here was the plan she'd promised: Send your husband an overseas telegram. Tell him you need money desperately. He'll send it at once. Maybe he'll even get a leave and come. Pay your mother back. Never come anywhere near Cleveland again.

That should take care of everything.

Chapter 11

Lulu rode around to the rear entrance of the squashed-looking apartment building. She took the stairs two at a time. If Mrs. Wysocki caught her, it would all be over.

But she made it to the third floor and knocked softly on 3-E. No response. She knocked again, a little harder, but still no one came. She put her ear to the door. It was as still as church in there.

"Tilda," she called quietly, "it's me. Lulu Leone Duckworth-Greene."

She heard the locks clicking and the bolt sliding. The door opened a slit, and one long gray eye peered out.

"What do you want?"

"You've got everything all wrong."

"Ha! Big shot! You got what you wanted, didn't you?"

"No, I didn't. All I wanted was to play a good game."

The slit widened an inch. Now Lulu could see two gray eyes.

"Game?"

"I got this fortune, and it said I had hidden resources, and I was hoping—"

"Lulu? Is that you, dearie?"

At the sound of Mrs. Wysocki's voice panting up the stairs, Tilda threw open her door and shot out her long, powerful arm. Before Mrs. Wysocki could make it to the landing, the locks and bolt were back in place, and Lulu once more had Jenny shinnying up her leg.

"Datsun, Datsun, Datsun," she crooned, and Lulu had no choice but to pick her up. "Oh, Datsun," she murmured, and yanked a handful of Lulu's hair.

"Sh!" Lulu put a finger to the baby's lips.

"Lulu? Are you in there or not?"

This time it was as if they were all in a play and knew their parts perfectly. Lulu, Tilda, and Jenny stayed absolutely still while Mrs. Wysocki tried a couple more times and then gave up.

"I'm losing my marbles over this," they heard her mutter as her slippers slapped back downstairs.

Jenny pulled the baseball cap off Lulu's head. She examined it carefully, trying to poke her fingers through the little holes on the top. Tilda fastened Lulu with her steely squint.

"What were you saying about a fortune?"

"I got it in a cookie. 'Hidden resources are at your command.' I thought it meant I was going to start playing better ball. That's the only thing I ever wanted to be a hero at."

"Then why'd you tell everyone about Jenny?"

"I didn't! Mrs. Wysocki did!"

Tilda's eyes narrowed even more. "Really?"

"I couldn't stop her."

"That sounds like her all right."

"I keep telling everyone it was just an accident, but nobody believes me. They keep asking me questions and trying to take my picture. They even want me to be on TV! The only thing I ever wanted to be good at was ball."

"Ball," agreed Jenny, and tried the cap on. It slid down over her eyes, and she laughed.

"What team do you root for?" Tilda asked suspiciously.

"There's only one team."

"Not the Indians."

"Who else?"

"They're losers! They stink!"

"They do not! This year's going to be different!"

Tilda tossed her hair. She put her big hands on her bony hips. "Just because they won yesterday doesn't mean—"

"What was the score?" Lulu realized that she'd been so busy reading about herself this morning, she hadn't even turned to the sports page.

"Six to five in the eleventh."

"They had to go into extra innings? But they were way ahead!"

"The Yanks tied it in the bottom of the eighth. I thought, oh no. Here we go again. I got that really sick feeling in the pit of my stomach. But then that tenth inning! That one double play—" Tilda's pale face lit up. She raised her eyes, as if the game were replaying in the air over Lulu's head. "Bert Watson. That guy's magic.

The play was like—you know. Ballet. Everybody in exactly the right place at the right time, and the whole
thing just—you know. Flowing."

Lulu was astonished. She had never heard another
girl talk that way about baseball. In fact, she'd never
heard *anyone* talk that way about it. But it was exactly
the way she felt about the game.

"I wish I'd seen it," she said. "Bert Watson—he's my
favorite player."

Tilda's gaze dropped to her face. "Swear you won't
tell!"

Not more swearing! Lulu thought. "Tell what?" she
asked.

"That I was listening to the game, and I forgot to
check on Jenny, and that's why she fell out the window!"

"She didn't fall, she jumped!"

"It doesn't make any difference! Shoot! What do you
care? You're the hero! But how do you think this makes
me look? Like a—you know. Terrible, rotten, no-good
mother, that's how!"

"Oh." Lulu had never thought of that. "But anybody
who knew Jenny would see she's awfully hard to
watch."

"Watch!" Jenny said from inside the cap.

"Nobody could blame you for taking a few minutes
off. Especially to listen to a game like that one."

"That's what you think! People blame mothers for
everything! If your kid does something wrong, it's always your fault."

This was news to Lulu. "That's not how my mother is," she said.

"You don't know. You're still a kid."

"You're not that old."

"I'm eighteen. That's old enough."

"For what?"

"You know what I thought when I was your age? I can't believe how stupid I was! I thought I'd grow up to be a major league pitcher. I thought I'd take the best offer, but I hoped I'd play for the Tribe. Ha! That's how stupid I was!"

"But the Tribe's on a roll! They're—"

"I don't mean it was stupid to want to play for the Tribe. Shoot, I was an Indian fan when you were still in Pampers! I mean it was stupid to think I could play, period!"

"Huh?"

"You may not have noticed, Lulu, but I'm a girl."

"So what?"

"How many girls do the Indians field?"

"But there's lots of girls on my Little League team. Well, not lots, but our best pitcher is a g—"

"Little League! When I was in Little League, I had to go twelve miles away because our town was so stupid and dinky, they didn't let girls play. And my mother wouldn't drive me because she said it wasn't a ladylike sport. She really said that! My mother never came to one game. Not even when they let me on varsity when I was only in tenth grade. She always said she couldn't get off work, but she—you know. She could've tried!"

Lulu took another look at Tilda. She saw that those long, sinewy muscles belonged to an athlete, all right. It was easy to imagine Tilda's mile-long legs sliding into second, or one of her windmill-blade arms swinging up and plucking a line drive—just the way a magician plucks a coin from thin air.

"Wow," said Lulu.

"Wow," said Jenny through the cap. She settled her head, cap and all, on Lulu's shoulder.

"Wow what? So what? I worked to be the best I could, and where did it get me?"

"My mother says women can do whatever they want."

"People lie."

"How about your husband? What does he say?"

Tilda turned away quickly, her baby-fine hair fanning out to hide her face. "He—he doesn't care much about baseball."

Then how can you love him? Lulu wanted to ask, but she didn't. Things were already complicated enough without trying to understand something as mysterious as grown-up love.

"By now my mother's read the paper. Or some nosy neighbor's come running over to show it to her. I've got thirty-six hours at the most before she runs me down."

She made her mother sound like a tractor trailer. As she spoke, Tilda somehow did seem to flatten out.

"She could have me arrested. But she probably won't. If I went to jail, who'd she have to pick on?"

"If only your husband—"

"Shoot! I told you, he's far away! Half the world away! I can't be counting on him for anything. Stop bringing him up."

"Mama," Jenny whimpered. She had fallen asleep on Lulu's shoulder. She smelled like vanilla. "Mama," she said again.

"Put her down," said Tilda. She made a limp gesture toward the bedroom.

Lulu had never put a baby to bed before. She never baby-sat because babies, even normal ones, made her very nervous. Now as she crossed the living room, she held her breath, afraid she'd drop Jenny or wake her up. And sure enough, the second she hit the mattress, Jenny began to cry.

"Mama!"

"It's okay. It's all right. Datsun's here. Datsun!"

Jenny looked at her with one eye.

"Go to sleep for Datsun, okay?"

The baby was still wearing the baseball cap. Now she dragged it off her head, put the visor in her mouth, shut her eyes, and began to snore.

Lulu let out a sigh of relief and looked around the room. That must be Tilda's bed—the table next to it was covered with *Sports Illustrated* and *Baseball Digest.* There were toys all over the place, most of them looking brand new. No wonder Tilda was broke. She hadn't thought about making a budget until it was too late.

The little room was very hot, and Lulu saw that the window was shut. Tiptoeing to it, she looked down through the frayed screen to the spot on the sidewalk where yesterday she'd stood yelling *no!*

It was a long way down, and there was no mistaking that rough concrete for a pillow. But maybe Jenny hadn't been thinking about where she'd land. Maybe instead she'd been noticing—the way Lulu was now— how soft the summer afternoon air looked. Maybe she'd been thinking she'd take a little ride on it, like that bit of white fluff, a petal or feather, drifting by.

And then she saw me. Yelling and making faces, doing the funniest dance she'd ever seen. What Jenny'd really wanted to do was play with that silly big girl down there. *Push on the screen, hurray!* She was strong! She could get out! Out of this hot, closed-up little place, with the mother who was so crabby and so worried and always saying no! Out into the sweet fresh air and dow-w-w-n. . . .

Lulu gripped the windowsill. For a split second, she'd felt as if she were falling too. The sidewalk, her hands and feet, the bricks of the building, and the blue of the sky all were jumbled up, like pieces of a puzzle tossed in the air. There was no up or down, no left or right, no me and them—nothing was the way it was supposed to be, and the danger took her breath away. For that second, she'd almost thought she *had* jumped.

"Psst!" Tilda stood in the doorway hissing.

Lulu crossed the room and quietly closed the door behind her.

"What are you smiling at?" Tilda demanded.

"Huh?"

"Did you notice the window's locked now? She's not going to fall out again. We'll just die of heat stroke, that's all."

Window locked. Heat stroke. Right. Lulu blinked, feeling her feet back on the ground.

"I can't believe how Jenny behaves for you. She's never that good for me. I think she jumped out that window to get away from me."

Lulu blinked again. Never before had she known what it was like to be inside someone else's skin.

"The first thing she did this morning was climb out of her crib and run to the window, saying, 'Datsun! Where are you, Datsun?' Then she started crying."

Sure she'd cried. For the first time in her life, Lulu felt —what did they call it when you couldn't stand to be cooped up? Claustrophobia. The walls of this tiny, melting-hot apartment seemed to be moving closer, like the walls in a horror movie. Sure Jenny had cried! She'd wanted to fly again! Didn't everybody secretly want to fly?

"I told Wysocki I was going," Tilda was saying, "but she wouldn't give me back my money. And what's the use? My mother will run me down no matter where I go. Besides, I can't keep moving Jenny around. Little kids are supposed to have—you know."

"Security."

"Yeah."

Lulu saw Tilda's mother, who would be really big, as big as a smokestack. Back in their small town, she would be telling everyone what a disappointment her daughter was, how she must have gotten the wrong baby in the hospital. "How did a woman like me end up with a kid like her?" she'd demand, and everyone would shake their heads in sympathy. She would just flatten Tilda like a pancake. And Jenny—what would happen to her?

"You can't go back home," Lulu said. It was exactly the opposite of what she'd come here planning to say. As soon as the words were out, she saw what she was getting herself into. But it was already too late.

Tilda paused. After a moment she said very quietly, "Where else can I go?"

Grammie would call it the $64,000 question. Lulu's fingers closed in fists. She felt as if she were starting to fall again.

It's up to me.

Her knees should have started to knock again. But they didn't. Instead, her fingers began to tingle. Her hands felt the way they had when she knew she was about to get a piece of it. Not the usual awful, stinging feeling. But that rare, breathtaking feeling when she connected.

"Is Tilda your real name?"

"Matilda Hubbard. It's almost as bad as yours."

"Then your mother probably will run you down without any trouble. You've got to disappear."

"Ha! You have some Disappearing Juice?"

"No, but I have a place for you to hide."

Tilda froze. "You do?"

"Not for long. Just till we can come up with a plan."

"I can be packed in an hour."

"Good. That's about how long it'll take me to make the arrangements."

Tilda strode to the door and undid the locks and bolt. "This hideout—does it have electricity?" she asked.

"Of course it does."

"I just wanted to make sure I could listen to the—you know. Game."

"See you in an hour."

Lulu flew down the stairs without making a sound. It didn't matter that she had no idea where she was going. As she grabbed her bike, her hands still tingled. She felt as if she'd rounded first and was lifting her head to see the outfielders still scrambling after her ball. She felt powerful. She felt amazed. She didn't feel like Lulu Leone Duckworth-Greene at all.

She'd ridden two whole blocks before the feeling began to fade. That was when she realized she'd left her baseball cap with Jenny. Her cap! Lulu never went anywhere without it. She felt bald. She felt naked. And where was she going, anyway? Her bike wobbled, and so did her heart, when she realized what she'd just done. She'd promised to save Tilda.

She'd acted as if she really *were* a hero.

Chapter 12

"Lulu!" Grammie looked up from her roast beef sandwich (white bread, hold the mayo). "I'd almost given up on seeing you today." She tore a little ridge of fat from the meat and fed it to Edward.

Everything was exactly the way Lulu had known it would be on a Sunday afternoon at Grammie's: cold sandwiches from the noon roast, the gospel music program on the radio, all the coupons clipped from the morning paper in a neat pile next to the toaster. Lulu's bike had seemed to find its own way here, to the one place on earth where everything was just the same as yesterday. Lulu slid into her seat at the table.

"Can I have some, Grammie?"

"Since when do you have to ask?"

They sat across from each other, eating the sandwiches and drinking milk. The gospel choir sang "Weep No More!" Grammie brought out a cold peach pie and cut Lulu a big slab. There was ice cream, too, the golden vanilla kind that was Lulu's favorite and that Elena never bought because it had artificial coloring in it. Lulu realized she hadn't eaten anything since the avocado omelet. As she ate, she began to relax for the first time in twenty-four hours. For Grammie, it was just like any old Sunday afternoon. As Lulu bent to give Edward her piecrust, the phone rang.

"Hello, Ellie. . . . Yes, she's here. Don't you feed the child? She's eating like a trencherman. . . . She's never fussy at my house. . . . All right, all right, calm down now. I'll tell her."

Grammie hung up. As she filled the kettle at the sink, she said, "Your mother was about to call the police on you, grandchild. You told her you'd be back in half an hour, and it's been five times that." She put the kettle on the stove and sat back down. "That's not like you."

"I know."

"Come to think of it, you look different."

Lulu rubbed her bare head. "My cap," she said.

"That's what it is. Say, how do you like that Tribe? If Doc Watson can only get himself some decent relief pitching, we're contenders for sure."

They discussed the Indians' chances as the tea water heated. *Just a plain old Sunday afternoon,* Lulu told herself. But then Grammie got up for the teacups.

"That was a fine thing you did yesterday, grandchild."

So she did know. There was no getting away from what had happened, not even at Grammie's.

"I didn't mean to do it. It was an accident."

Grammie nodded slowly. "I wondered about that," she said. "You never were much for derring-do." She set the cups on the table. "I wondered if it was just a chance thing, like being struck by lightning."

Lulu drank her milky sweet tea, then said good-bye. As she got back on her bike, she knew Grammie had hit the nail on the head.

But then, what was it she'd read once about lightning's effect on the people it struck?

The sun stood on the horizon. Its rays struck Lulu straight in the chest, turning her T-shirt to spun gold. Before she'd gone a whole block, she turned her bike around.

"Grammie," she said, coming back into the house. Grammie, at the sink, turned in surprise. "I have to ask you something."

Chapter 13

"Don't worry. I didn't tell her who you were or anything. I just told her I met somebody who needed a place to stay for a little while, and since she has two empty bedrooms and my mother's always telling her she needs someone to watch out for her—"

"I can't watch out for an old lady! I can't even watch out for me and Jenny!"

"Grammie's not an old lady! She's—you know. A person."

They were almost in sight of Grammie's house. Tilda was pushing Jenny's stroller and carrying an enormous suitcase. Shopping bags hung from the stroller handles, and Lulu staggered under a box bursting with toys. They'd had to leave the crib behind. All the other stuff went with the apartment, which Tilda had rented furnished.

"And good riddance!" she'd hissed as they snuck down the back stairs.

But now she set down the suitcase and wouldn't go another step.

"Why should she let me in? She doesn't even know me. And wait till she sees Jenny. You said she likes peace and quiet."

"Grammie will love Jenny." Lulu, reaching down to give Jenny a pat on the head, surreptitiously tried to slip her baseball cap off. "Such a cute little—"

"Grrr!" Jenny bared her teeth and clamped a hand over the cap. "Mine, Datsun!" she said fiercely.

"Wait'll the first time Jenny does her tornado-warning imitation. Or eats the centerpiece. Or pees on the rug. Or—"

"It'll be okay," said Lulu. She ran a hand over the top of her head, longing for her cap back. Grammie's idea of a commotion was Edward giving two halfhearted barks at the mail carrier. But now that they'd snuck all Tilda's stuff out of the apartment, there was no turning back. Grammie had said, sure she'd like to meet Lulu's friends. But little did she know Lulu wanted those friends to *live* with her. If she wouldn't take them in, where would they go? Could Lulu hide them in her garage? She'd have to smuggle food out to them in the middle of the night, and—

"Want out," said Jenny, pulling at the stroller strap. "Want out!"

"Not yet," said Tilda.

"Want out!" yelled Jenny, banging her feet.

Sure she'd hide them in the garage. She might as well try to hide the Ohio State marching band. Lulu shifted the heavy box of toys.

I'm carrying more than just toys.

"It's never going to work," said Tilda.

"Yes, it will," said Lulu.

"You should know. You're the *hero.*"

She made it sound like a dirty four-letter word. She had a way of twisting her mouth that could make *love* sound like a curse. By now the toys in the box were so heavy, they seemed made of lead.

Side by side they trudged on. It was night now, and the lighted windows looked like cutouts stuck to black paper. Past one, a woman carried a baby in pajamas. Someone whistled for his dog. Suddenly, a snatch of Indians game floated out on the dark, and both Tilda and Lulu stood stock-still.

"Breaking ball—swung on and missed—strike three!" Then a beer commercial came on.

They trudged on. They could hear supper dishes being washed, and someone playing a flute. Lulu thought that if Grammie wouldn't take them in, they'd have to walk all night long past windows like these. They'd have to spend the whole night on the outside looking in.

But it wasn't true. Lulu wasn't an outcast. If she wanted, she could drop this box of toys and run. She had a home to run to and parents waiting for her—even if it was a home with power tools lying all over the living room, and even if the waitress who called them Happy Family had to have been severely nearsighted. Lulu had them. They were hers.

Not Tilda.

"There's Grammie's," she said, pointing two houses ahead.

"Want out!" Jenny yelled. She banged her heels so hard the stroller shook. "Wantoutwantoutwantout-wantout!"

"Okay, okay! You can walk the rest of the way." Tilda undid the stroller strap. Jenny sprang to her feet and took off—unfortunately, into the street. Tilda grabbed her, and Jenny bit her hand.

"Yeow!"

"Waaaah!"

"Don't cry, Jenny, are you all right, Tilda, it'll be okay, don't cry," said Lulu. A run-on sentence. "It'll be okay!"

"No, it won't!" said Tilda, picking up the baby. Jenny

cried, "Datsun!" and leaped into Lulu's arms, knocking the toys all over the sidewalk. Tilda displayed the teeth marks on the back of her hand.

"It won't be anywhere near okay. If your grandmother has the IQ of a houseplant, she won't even let us up her front walk."

"You always think the worst of people," Lulu burst out. "What's the matter with you?"

Tilda glared at her with steely gray eyes. She sucked the back of her hand and didn't reply.

Lulu set Jenny down on the sidewalk.

"Help me pick these up," she said to the baby, and began to put the toys back in the box. As soon as she put something in, Jenny took it back out. Tears pushed at the back of Lulu's eyes. All night long into the dawn they'd have to trudge, with Tilda complaining and Jenny yelling and all the responsibility on her, Lulu Leone Duckworth-Greene. *Hero* really *was* a dirty word! All night long—and then what?

Next to the toy box, the toe of Tilda's enormous hightop dug in the dirt.

"I know you know everything. A hero's supposed to know everything."

The tears pushed so hard at the backs of Lulu's eyes, one got out. Suddenly, Tilda crouched down beside her.

"You know everything, and you think something's the matter with me," she hissed. "Like what?"

Lulu knew Tilda didn't really care what a pipsqueak like her thought. She just wanted to make sure Lulu didn't get away with insulting her. So Lulu said the first thing that popped into her head.

"Didn't you ever notice which way your nose points?"

"What?"

"Never mind."

"I want to know what you said."

"It's just one of my mother's sayings. 'Did you ever notice which way your nose points?'" Lulu put the Cabbage Patch with the crayoned face back in the box. "And 'Your eyes are in the front of your head, not the back.' She means people should expect good stuff out of life. She's always saying it to me."

"Shoot! See how lucky you are?"

"Lucky? Me?"

"Having a mother who says funny things like that. *Smart* funny things. My mother's idea of funny is—you know. Somebody slipping on a banana peel and breaking their neck."

"Everybody always likes my mother. That doesn't mean I'm lucky."

Tilda picked up a naked Barbie doll. "What do you mean?"

"My mother's funny, like you said. She has muscles like a trapeze artist, and last winter she read *War and Peace*—the whole thing. She looks like Cher, only with short red hair. People always meet her and say 'Wow!'"

"See how lucky you are?"

"They look at her and say 'Wow!' Then they look at me and say 'Oh.'"

Tilda sat back on her heels. "Oh," she said. "I get it."

"I don't care what other people think. I mean, if you grow up with a name like Lulu Leone Duckworth-Greene, you get used to ignoring stuff. But—" Lulu picked up a teething ring. She felt like biting it. "I wish she wasn't always disappointed in me."

"You must hate her."

"I—"

"You must get so mad, you want to kick her. Bite her. Punch her out!" Tilda hurled the Barbie doll into the box.

"I don't get mad very much. Just worried."

"But that must all be different now that you're a hero."

"It's not. She wants me to be on TV, on *Stars of the Heights,* and I won't."

Tilda's eyes narrowed to silver slits. "Because I made you swear not to betray me?"

"Not only that. I don't want to be on TV. For one thing, I'll just stutter the whole time. My ears will get all red. I'll look ridiculous on color TV. And besides, I'm really not a hero. I keep trying to tell her, this whole thing was just an accident. I'm—"

"Hey." Tilda reached over and grabbed the neck of Lulu's T-shirt. Lulu thought she was going to choke her again. But Tilda's eyes grew wide and luminous, like lakes in the moonlight. "You told me to stop talking like that," she said. "Now I'm telling you."

Lulu looked into Tilda's silver eyes, and she knew why Tilda's husband had fallen in love with her. Lakes in the moonlight—anyone would want to dive right in. Not only was Tilda a baseball star, she was beautiful.

And she believes in me.

"Okay," Lulu said, and the way the word came out, it had three syllables instead of two.

"Okay," Tilda said, and pulled Lulu to her feet.

"Oday!" Jenny said, and grabbing a stuffed dinosaur from the toy box, charged down the sidewalk.

"It's right there," Lulu said, pointing two houses down. Grammie stood in her doorway.

"Dr. Livingstone, I presume," Grammie said, and swung open the screen.

"Grammie, this is . . . um . . ." Why hadn't they thought to make up aliases? "This is . . . um . . ."

"Datsun!" said Jenny, diving past Grammie's legs.

"Datsun! That's right. Datsun Watson and her mother Bertie."

"It's short for Alberta," said Tilda, extending her hand. Grammie shook it.

"I'm pleased to meet you. Come on in, Bertie."

They left the suitcases and toys on the porch and went into the kitchen. Jenny was already there, sitting on Edward's back and pulling his ears. Edward looked ready to have a dog heart-attack.

"Jenny! No, no!" Tilda rushed toward her, but Jenny jumped up and ran out of the room. Crash!

It was the cut-glass candy dish that Grammie always kept on her sideboard. Jenny crawled among the shards of glass, picking up the buttermints and popping them into her mouth.

"No, no!" yelled Tilda again. Now she was the one who looked on the verge of a heart attack.

"*No, no* is right," Grammie said calmly and, hoisting Jenny up by the seat of her overalls, set the baby in a chair. "Now, you stay right there and don't move." She went out and returned with her dustpan and broom.

"I'll do it!" cried Tilda. "I'm so sorry!"

"You just watch that baby of yours," said Grammie, kneeling down stiffly.

Tilda gave Lulu a despairing look. Jenny stood up on her chair and reached for a wax apple, which she began to gnaw.

"I told you!" whispered Tilda. "I told you she'd eat the centerpiece!" She grabbed the apple from Jenny, who of course began to howl. "No, no!" cried Tilda again.

Grammie pulled herself up on the back of a chair. "*No, no* doesn't work with that variety, Bertie," she said sternly. "Datsun, come on with me. I've got a chore for you."

Jenny stopped midhowl. Scrambling down from her chair, she followed Grammie into the kitchen.

"Now, we're going to have some refreshments," Grammie said, and handed her a plastic glass. At the sight of the baby, Edward got up and left the room as quickly as his fat old legs would carry him.

"You put one glass by each chair," said Grammie.

Jenny ran around setting out the glasses.

"Now napkins."

"Nappins."

"Good job, Datsun. Now, climb up on your chair, and we'll see if we have any cookies."

Jenny climbed into a chair. She folded her hands in her lap. Tilda passed a hand over her face.

"Sit down, Bertie," said Grammie. "My guess is you've had a long day."

They all sat down, and Grammie poured out Cokes for the three of them and milk for Jenny.

"Here's your cookie, Datsun."

"Dank you," said Jenny politely.

Tilda slumped as if she'd witnessed a miracle. "I'm sorry about that dish," she began. "I'll buy you a new one."

"It's not the first time a baby's broken something in this house. Though it's been a long time. Dependable Dan here never did anything like that. I could've left her alone in a room full of Waterford crystal without worrying. It was her mother who gave me a run for my money."

Jenny was crumbling her cookie into approximately ten thousand pieces, but Grammie didn't seem to notice.

"Grammie's my mother's mother," said Lulu.

"Gammie," said Jenny, decimating another chunk.

"That's right," said Grammie, looking at her. "And you're Datsun. Young people sure come up with distinctive names these days."

"It's an old family name," said Tilda.

"I see," said Grammie. "And this is Edward," she

went on, as the dog cautiously reappeared. "Say 'Edward,' Datsun."

"Eddord," said Jenny, and showered cookie crumbs all over the dog's head.

"No, no!" cried Tilda again, jumping up. "Don't get up, Grammie! I know where the dustpan is."

Jenny threw her arms around Edward's neck as the dog licked the floor.

"She—she's really not as wild as she seems," said Lulu. "Well, I mean, she is kind of wild, but mostly she's just curious."

"Curious George. That's what we used to call your mother, you know."

Then Grammie smiled, and Lulu could see she was going to tell one of her stories about Elena. They were the only stories Grammie ever told.

"Bertie, it goes against my grain to give advice, but from my first look at that baby, I could see you were in trouble. When Lulu's mother was just a little bigger, she took a bus to Akron."

"Akron!" cried Tilda, trying to stop Jenny from licking up the crumbs alongside Edward.

"That's right. We were at the bus station to meet my brother. He lived in Pittsburgh then. Somehow she got away from me and waltzed herself up on that bus. Everybody thought she belonged to somebody else. That was when she was two, mind you. Imagine for yourself what I had to put up with by the time she was fifteen."

"I can see Jen—Datsun doing that."

"At least she doesn't suck her thumb, does she? Elena

was four and wouldn't stop. Her father put hot pepper on it. She licked it off and begged for more. When she was six, she fell off the roof. I looked up from the kitchen sink, and there she went, tumbling by. She landed in my laundry basket. That variety counts on miracles."

Lulu and Tilda exchanged looks. Grammie sipped her Coke and shook her head. Lulu couldn't remember the last time she'd heard Grammie talk so much.

"It wears me out just remembering what I went through with that girl. Her father always said, 'She's as full of life as an egg is meat.' He loved her to distraction." Grammie smiled again. "But then he died when she was just ten. I was the one who did most of the raising. The day she got married, I went down on my knees and said, 'Thank goodness she's off my hands!' "

Jenny was hugging Edward so hard, the dog's eyes looked ready to pop out. Grammie lifted her into her lap and handed her a napkin, which the baby immediately began to shred.

Lulu cleared her throat. "Grammie, Bertie and Datsun need a place to stay."

Grammie took a sip of Coke. "Is that so," she said.

"Just for a couple of weeks."

"Just passing through, are you?"

Tilda sat down. She wrapped a leg around a chair rung. "We—you know."

Lulu watched Grammie look at Tilda, and she saw the fine line between Grammie's eyes deepen.

"No, I don't know," said Grammie. "We what?"

"What," said Jenny.

"We—we're finding our way."

The line deepened. Grammie took off the baseball cap and began to redo one of Jenny's pigtails.

"I have only one room. It's too small for a family."

"It's just the two of them," said Lulu. "Till—I mean, Bertie's husband's in the navy."

Grammie raised her eyes, and Lulu saw a look she didn't understand pass between her and Tilda. When Tilda spoke again, it was in a whisper.

"That's right. Just the two of us."

Grammie fingered Jenny's pigtail. "For fifteen years it was just me and my daughter. Two's all it takes to make a family. What do you do, Bertie?"

"Do?"

"For a living."

"I . . . um . . . you know. I—"

"You can tell her," said Lulu. "Bertie's unemployed, Grammie."

"I see," said Grammie.

"I see," said Jenny.

"But I'm going to get a job!" cried Tilda, jumping up from her chair. "Starting tomorrow, I'm going on interviews. I'm starting over. I'm getting up at dawn, and I'm not coming back till I—you know. Get hired."

"Who's going to mind Curious George here?"

"I am," Lulu heard herself say.

Grammie looked from one to the other. Her mouth was frowning, but her eyes began to laugh as if someone was tickling her behind her knees.

"So, you two have it all figured out," she said.

"Out," said Jenny. She grabbed the baseball cap and slipped off Grammie's lap. Going to the kitchen door, she pressed her nose against the screen. "Light," she said, and they all looked to see the firefly drifting up into the night sky.

"Magics," said Grammie. "That's what Ellie used to call them."

"What do you think, Gram?"

"I think I never saw you so heated up about anything outside of baseball, grandchild." She looked at Tilda. "As far as I can remember, Lulu's only introduced me to one other friend. And by the way, how'd that baby get your baseball cap? I thought you only took it off to shower."

"She just took it. Now she won't give it back."

Grammie nodded slowly. "I know this variety."

"It'd only be for a couple of weeks, Gram. Till Bertie gets stuff together. She'll start to pay you as soon as she gets a job."

"I'll pay you, you know. Interest," said Tilda.

"What do you think?"

"I think that room's been closed up for a long time. It's going to take a lot of cleaning and airing."

"We'll do it!" Lulu threw her arms around her grandmother. "I'll call Mom right now and tell her I won't be home for a while yet."

Grammie gave a chuckle. "Your mom's going to be very pleased. She's been pestering me for months now to get someone in that room. She thinks I need someone to look after me, Alberta. She's the one needs looking after, I keep saying. But she wins again, as usual."

"Gammie." Turning from the screen, Jenny came and wedged herself between Grammie's knees. Her small fat hand flashed out, and she almost snatched Grammie's glasses off her nose. But Grammie was faster and, catching her, pulled the baby into her lap.

"Monkey," she said.

"Monkey."

"I'll keep her out of your way," said Tilda. "I won't let her bother you, I promise."

"I thought it was Dependable Dan here who was going to be the baby-sitter."

Lulu, dialing the phone, felt her hands begin to tingle again. "That's right!" she said.

Chapter 14

Tilda and Lulu aired and cleaned the spare room, which—tidy as Grammie was—hardly needed it at all. They got the crib down from the attic, and Tilda had it together in a flash. She found a piece of sandpaper in the basement and smoothed a few splintery spots.

"Are you good at fixing stuff too?" Lulu asked her.

Tilda tossed her a suspicious look. "What do you mean, *too?*"

"You said you're good at baseball. Are you good at fixing stuff too?"

Tilda tightened one last screw. "There," she said.

Grammie brought Jenny, fresh from a bath, into the room. She was still wearing the baseball cap.

"I couldn't get it off her, not for a second."

"Datsun!" Jenny said, and climbed into the crib. "Night night!" she yelled, and began to bounce up and down.

"I'll leave that monkey to you," Grammie told Tilda. "I have to drive Lulu home. It's almost ten o'clock." She went downstairs.

Tilda grabbed Lulu's T-shirt. "Will you really come baby-sit for me tomorrow?"

"I said I would."

"Come as early as you can. I meant what I said. If I can find a job, I can start saving money to pay my mother back. I'll give her interest too. If I can find something good, I won't have to be afraid of her any-more. I can start over and show her I can—you know. Provide for Jenny. Do it on my own."

"Beep beep!" Jenny imitated the sound of Grammie's car horn.

"I'll be here," Lulu said.

Both her parents were in the living room when she walked in. Elena was doing a yoga headstand, and

David, his feet propped on the industrial vacuum in the middle of the floor, was watching TV.

"There you are!" Elena flipped herself right-side up. "That must have been the longest bike ride on record!"

"Hi, Mom. Hi, Dad."

David got up and switched off the TV. "How's the hero doing?"

Lulu tried to give a casual shrug. "Okay, I guess. But I'm pretty tired, so good night." She started for the stairs, but Elena gave a whoop.

"Not so fast, pardner. Where have you been all day?"

Lulu tried to shrug again, but this time her shoulders seemed to get stuck up by her ears. "Oh, you know."

Elena looked interested. "What's that supposed to mean? Are you keeping a secret from us, lambchop?"

"Lulu doesn't keep secrets," said David.

"I know," said Elena, looking even more interested.

"I called you. I was helping Grammie's new roomer move in."

"Where'd this new roomer suddenly come from?"

"Oh, I don't know. Just out of the blue." It wasn't a lie. The sky had been very blue yesterday, when Jenny jumped.

"Curiouser and curiouser."

"She and Grammie just sort of found each other. Anyway, I have to go back and help again in the morning, so I better get to bed. You know I need eight hours' sleep."

But Elena slipped an arm around Lulu's shoulders. She smelled like paint thinner and the strawberry bubble gum she was chewing. Her red hair was staticky from her headstand. She blew a bubble—*pop!*

"You're not acting like yourself at all," she told Lulu happily.

If only you knew, thought Lulu.

"You got two more important calls after you left. One was from that reporter—the pushy one that looks like an alligator? I guess she wants to do a follow-up story, and she's been trying all day to get in touch with that baby's mother. Finally, tonight she went over, and she and Mrs. Wysocki knocked and knocked, but nobody answered, so Mrs. Wysocki got her key. Guess what?" Elena blew an enormous bubble—*pop!* "They're gone! Booked! Isn't that bizarre?"

"Huh? Bizarre? What's so bizarre about it?"

"First she lets her baby fall out a window, then she skips town the very next day? You know I'm not judgmental, but she doesn't exactly sound stable to me. It makes you worry about the poor baby."

"You don't need to worry about her. That baby can take care of herself! She's fine."

"I thought you said you didn't get to know them."

"I didn't. I just mean . . ."

"It's all very strange. Even her name—what was her name again?"

"Bertie. No, I mean Tilda! What's so strange about it? It's not any stranger than my weird name!"

"Your name's not weird, lambchop." Elena drew Lulu close again. "It's an old, old name. In fact, it's a diminutive of Louis. A very *regal* name."

"I guess I should be glad you didn't name me Henry VIII."

"Or Richard the Lionhearted." David gave a tug on Lulu's braid. "Hey, where's your cap?"

"I guess I left it at Grammie's."

"I hardly recognize you without it. Lulu is to her baseball cap what Elena is to her belt sander."

"Bleagh." Elena crossed her eyes and stuck out her tongue. "That was your other call. Coach Angell. There's a practice tomorrow at three."

"Okay. I really better get to bed now."

"Good night, Lu," said David. "Sleep tight."

But Elena caught the belt loop of Lulu's jeans as she started for the stairs.

"Did you think anymore about being on *Stars of the Heights?*"

Lulu nodded.

Elena's amber eyes lit up. "You did?"

"Yeah. I don't want to."

The lights went out.

"If I didn't want you to, you would," said Elena.

"El . . ." said David.

"Never mind." Elena crossed the room and flipped her feet up on the wall.

Chapter 15

The next morning Lulu got up very early and left this note on the kitchen table:

> *Went to help Grammie with her new roomer. Will probably go straight to practice. See you for supper.*
>
> Love,
Lulu

She took two Rice Krispies, put them in a bowl, and poured three drops of milk on them. Then she set the bowl in the sink. If her mother thought she hadn't eaten breakfast, she'd get really suspicious, because Lulu never left the house without a bowl of Rice Krispies. Only today she didn't have time. Today, she realized, she wasn't even hungry. Today was not just any day.

Grammie had brought Lulu's bike home in the trunk of her car last night, and now she wheeled it out into the pale pink morning. Lulu had never been outside this early before. Dew beaded the spiderwebs in the grass and made them look like tiny, shimmering trampolines. Lulu imagined being tiny and light enough to bounce on one.

She looked up—what made her look up this time?—and saw a large bird flying over. The bird had long, thin legs that streamed behind like ribbons. It was the kind of bird she'd seen painted on Chinese scrolls, its wings edged in gold by the sunlight. What was its name? She didn't know.

She rode through the sleepy streets to Grammie's house. Tilda came out onto the steps, shutting the door silently behind her.

"Thanks for coming," she whispered.

She wore a pink dress with little pearl buttons all the way down the front. She'd added another set of earrings, pink crystal hearts, above the diamonds, and piled her hair high on her head. Her eyelids were ultramarine, and her cheeks frosty peach. Lulu thought she had never looked more beautiful.

"Grammie and Jenny are still asleep."

The paper boy rode by and flung a newspaper toward them. Lulu unfolded it and took out the want ads.

"Look at all these jobs. You're probably going to have a hard time deciding which one to take."

"Probably."

Tilda reached for the paper, and Lulu saw that her fingers were shaking like twigs in a hurricane. Lulu decided not to tell her about the reporter and Mrs. Wysocki discovering she was gone. Tilda had enough on her mind already. Besides, by tonight their troubles would be over. Lulu knew Tilda would find a good job.

One steely look from those gray eyes would convince anyone she could do anything.

Tilda opened the enormous purse slung from her shoulder, and something fell out. When Lulu picked it up, she saw it was a photo of Jenny in the snow. Her little face glowed beneath a dark wool cap. Tilda snatched it back.

"That's to keep me going," she said, slipping it into the purse with the want ads. "If my knees start to knock, I'll look at it."

"*Your* knees?" Lulu laughed. "That'll be the day."

"Yeah. Ha ha." Tilda laughed too. "I put Jenny's clothes out. Be strict with her. You have to be real strict."

"Okay."

"Grammie said you get the bus at that corner."

"Right."

"See you."

Tilda swung down the street.

Go, Tilda. Hit one out of the park.

Lulu felt wonderful. She sat on Grammie's front steps, watching how the sunlight inched up the tree on the tree lawn as if the trunk were a long gray fuse. At last the sun reached the leaves—a golden sparkler, suddenly lit! Each leaf was edged in gold, like the wings of that bird with the long legs. The air was gentle and pink, as up and down the street doors opened. People left for work or stuck out tousled heads to discover where the paper boy had landed the paper today. Lulu wondered how she could have spent so much of her life sleeping through summer mornings. What a waste! From now on, she'd get up at dawn. She wouldn't miss one second of this beautiful, fresh, new time of day. She opened Grammie's paper and read about the Indians' second glorious victory in a row.

"Look who's here!" Grammie, her bowling-ball bag in hand, stepped out onto the front porch. "Don't tell me Bertie's already gone!"

"She left a long time ago. Is Datsun still asleep?" Lulu folded the paper and stood up.

"One good thing about monkeys like her—they wear themselves out. Then sleep like logs. Today's my bowling day, you know. I'm meeting Anna for a cup of coffee, and then we're headed for the lanes."

"Okay. I hope you roll all strikes."

"I'll settle for not dropping the ball on my foot, thanks."

Lulu watched Grammie start to say something else, then stop. She knew Grammie wanted to ask, "Are you sure you can manage all this?" But Grammie didn't want to insult Lulu. She wanted to give her credit for knowing what she was capable of. Lulu had never loved her grandmother more.

"We'll be fine, Grammie," she said. "Jenny and I get along great."

"Jenny?"

"That's her middle name!"

"I see. I'll probably go to lunch with the girls afterward, so I might not be home till three."

"I'll be gone to practice. I'm sure Bertie'll be back way before then."

Grammie started toward the garage. "Just see that that monkey doesn't stick anything in the outlets. And keep an eye on the washer. One day your mother climbed into the machine and turned it on before I caught her."

Lulu watched Grammie back the car out. She waved good-bye, then went inside. From upstairs came a sudden large thud. Lulu ran up in time to see Jenny, in a diaper and the baseball cap, come flying out of the bedroom as if catapulted from a giant slingshot. She hugged Lulu's knees, then burst into heartbroken sobs.

"Mama! Mama!"

"Mama went to get a job," explained Lulu. Jenny paused an instant, then cried even harder. "No, no! It's okay! Mama will be back—she's only going to be gone a little while. A teensy-weensy while, Jenny. Datsun will take care of you."

Jenny gnawed on Lulu's knee. "Datsun, Mama?"

Lulu crouched down. Jenny pressed against her, and Lulu could feel her heart beating. She was so little, but she was a person, a whole person. A quiver of tenderness went through Lulu.

"You know what you need?" she said. "Breakfast."

"Brekkie," Jenny agreed, and wiped her runny nose on Lulu's T-shirt.

They went downstairs to the kitchen, and Lulu set the baby onto some pillows on a chair. She found the Rice Krispies that Grammie kept for when she slept over and filled a bowl. She poured on lots of milk because she knew little kids need lots of calcium for strong bones and teeth. In a drawer she found Elena's baby spoon and, proud of how easy all this was, set the breakfast in front of Jenny.

The baby looked from the bowl to Lulu and back to the bowl with delight. Then with one swipe of her hand she knocked the whole thing onto the linoleum.

"Wahoo!" she yelled.

The tenderness Lulu had been feeling evaporated immediately. As she knelt to clean the mess, Jenny patted her on the head. Rice Krispies had glued themselves to the chair legs and the bottoms of the cupboards. Milk was soaking a box of tissues Jenny had tossed onto the floor. The bowl lay in three neat pieces.

"You weren't supposed to do that, you know." Lulu tried to make her voice stern, remembering what Tilda had said about being strict.

"You know," Jenny said, and patted Lulu's head some more.

When she'd cleaned everything up, Lulu handed the baby a piece of bread and butter. Jenny shredded it and put the pieces in her hair. Lulu could see where this would begin to get on your nerves after a while. She set Jenny on the floor and told her to go play.

A mistake. A painful howl arose in the living room, and Lulu ran in to see Jenny trying to shove one of Edward's legs into Grammie's sweater.

"No, no! Stop it!"

Jenny dropped the sweater and began to cry.

"I'm sorry, I didn't mean to yell, but he's a dog, not a toy, plus he's old. You have to be gentle with him. Nice doggie, nice, nice!"

"Nice!" Jenny began to kiss Edward's nose. The dog squeezed his eyes shut like a child watching a monster movie.

"I can see I'll have to keep you in sight," Lulu told the baby. She took her upstairs and slipped on the sundress Tilda had left out. "Now, what do you want to play?"

"Rumm rumm," said Jenny, running to the box of toys.

So Lulu lay on the floor and pushed the red truck over to Jenny. Jenny pushed it back. Then they pushed the silver car. Every once in a while Jenny would pick one up and suck on it, so when Lulu got it, it was covered with drool.

"Ugh," Lulu said. "Yuck!"

"Yuck." Jenny laughed. Then she threw the truck at Lulu.

They played blocks, dolls, and stuffed animals. Lulu did a puppet show. She bounced Jenny on her foot. She sang "Old MacDonald" and "The Eentsy Weentsy Spider" five times each. Jenny was in ecstasy. She watched with wide eyes, waiting to see what Lulu would think of next.

"Aren't you getting tired? Don't you want a nap?"

"No no no no no!"

"Oh. How about some lunch then?"

Jenny tore down the stairs and into the kitchen. Lulu made her a peanut butter and jelly sandwich. Jenny peeled it apart and poked her fingers all through it, but this time she actually ate some. Lulu gave her a tiny bit of milk and sliced pieces of banana. Jenny smooshed them into her mouth with her palm.

Lulu herself was starving by now, but she was too tired to get up and make herself something. She'd never known what hard work it was to be a mother. Had Elena gone through days like this with her? Lulu knew she could never have been as much trouble as Jenny was, but all babies took a lot of work—she could see that now. They needed so much! You just had to keep giving them stuff, food and attention and guidance, and you didn't get very much back. A drooly car and a sticky pat on the head. Being a mother was sort of like being a hero.

Now, that was a funny thought.

Jenny gave a yawn, and Lulu felt hopeful. Maybe if she read to her, Jenny would fall asleep. She could still remember how heavy her own eyes used to get the minute her mother began to read *Good Night Moon.*

She searched through Jenny's books, but she couldn't find *Good Night Moon.* She chose *The Poky Little Puppy* instead. Taking Jenny on her lap, she began to read about the five mischievous puppies who were always going "roly-poly, pell-mell, tumble-bumble."

By the time she'd read the book three times—because Jenny kept shouting "again!"—her eyelids felt as if they had weights attached. Jenny, her dark eyes bright, bent to examine the puppies' bowl of chocolate custard. Lulu, just for a second, let her own eyes close. . . .

She was riding her bike to practice. A distant, squeaky voice cried, "Help! Save me!" She looked up, and there in the window was a tiny girl with a cereal bowl on her head and the want ads in her hand. "Datsun!" she called. "I need you!" Then she spread her arms and jumped. Her little legs streamed behind her like ribbons.

But this time Lulu didn't catch her. This time Jenny lifted Lulu, and they sailed off together. Lulu felt the baby's soft, downy hair against her cheek. Bells pealed far below. Warmth wrapped her from . . .

Lulu's eyes flew open. Her head had fallen back against her chair. A small pink blanket was draped over her. The phone was ringing, and Jenny was gone.

Chapter 16

It must be Tilda. Lulu couldn't let her suspect anything was wrong. She ran down the hall to Grammie's bedroom. Though her heart was hammering, she made her voice as normal as possible.

"Hello?"

"Hello. This is Sissy Potash. May I please speak to Lulu Leone Duckworth-Greene?"

"What? Who?"

"Pardon me?"

Jenny wasn't in Grammie's bedroom or in the hall. Lulu suddenly thought of the bathroom. Grammie always kept the window open in there. Lulu dropped the phone and ran back down the hall.

The baby lay curled up next to the tub, snoring, a tube of lipstick in her fist. Above her a wild, flamingo-colored mural sprawled across the wall.

"You rotten little kid!" yelled Lulu.

Jenny smiled in her sleep.

"Mama," she murmured. "Datsun."

Her heart still scrabbling to get out of her chest, Lulu crouched down beside the baby. She had lipstick all over her cheeks, and her eyelids were electric blue. On the floor beside her was more makeup than Lulu had ever seen anyplace outside of the Woolworth's counter —tubes, brushes, rectangles, and circles of lovely pearly color. Lulu didn't know what half of it was for. The smell was wonderful—just like Tilda. Jenny had probably been itching to get her hands on that makeup case forever.

"You rotten little kid," Lulu said again, in a whisper this time.

She went back out into the hall to look for Grammie's scrub brush. A funny, tinny little sound made her look toward Grammie's bedroom. The phone receiver lay on the floor where she'd dropped it.

"Hello? Hello?" someone cried in her ear. "Are you there?"

"Yes."

"Oh. You are? I thought we'd been disconnected. Who is this?"

"Who is *this*?"

"This is Sissy Potash, from the *Plain Dealer.* I need to speak to Lulu Leone Duckworth-Greene, please. It's very important."

Lulu recognized the voice of the reporter who'd followed her down the driveway and right up to the door the day she'd rescued Jenny—the reporter Elena had said looked like an alligator. David had had to shut the door in this reporter's face. Lulu's knees began to shake.

"Lulu . . . Lulu doesn't live here."

"I know. But I just spoke to her mother, and she said I could catch Lulu here. This is her grandmother's, isn't it?"

"Yes. But—"

"Is Lulu there?" Sissy Potash began to sound impatient. "It's very important that I speak to her. I need her help to contact Matilda Hubbard."

Lulu sank down to the floor. "Matilda Hubbard?"

"Yes," said the reporter, no longer trying to hide her impatience. "Matilda Hubbard."

"I heard a rumor that she left town."

"So did I. That's why I need Lulu's help. She's the

only one who ever really talked to Matilda here in Cleveland. She's the only one who might give us a clue to where she's gone."

"Wh—what do you need to know that for?"

"I have someone who desperately wants to contact her."

Lulu's voice came out in a croak. "Who?"

"That's confidential. Is Lulu there, please?"

"I—I can take a message for her."

"Fine. Tell her to call me as soon as possible. Here's the number." Sissy Potash dictated a number and extension. "Have you got that?"

"Yes."

"Can I ask who this is?"

"You can ask, but I won't tell you," Lulu said, and hung up.

Slowly she stood up and went back down the hall. She sat on the edge of the bathtub and watched Jenny sleep. Her father had once told her that when he was having a restless or troubled night, he'd come sit by her bed. "Watching you sleep," her father said, "always makes me feel peaceful."

But watching Jenny sleep didn't make Lulu feel peaceful. She was certain that the person who desperately wanted to see Tilda was Tilda's mother, the tractor trailer herself. Just as Tilda had predicted, she'd seen the newspaper story and gone running to the phone. She'd spoken to Sissy Potash. Sissy Potash knew a hot story when she heard one! First a cute little baby falls out a third-floor window. Not only does she survive, but it turns out her mother is a robber. A robber who disappears into thin air overnight.

What if Sissy Potash found out the rest of the story? That the supposed hero had helped the robber mother disappear? That the cute little baby was possessed? That the hero had duped her innocent grandmother into hiding a desperate fugitive from justice? What if Sissy Potash found out all that?

And where was Tilda? She should've been home long ago! It was almost time to leave for practice. She couldn't miss a practice only two days after missing a game. The plan had seemed so simple: find a job, pay back the tractor trailer, become a regular, respectable person. But when it came to Tilda and Jenny, it seemed, nothing was simple.

Lulu stood up. She had to do something. And the only thing she could think of was to go to practice.

She always did her best thinking with her glove on. Of all the reasons Lulu had thought of for why she loved baseball, she'd never thought of the one she did now: it was so *simple.* Baseball had clear, definite rules for every situation. You always knew what you were supposed to do next. There was never any doubt about anything. At any confusion, you just stepped back and let the umpires decide. Even when you were out, you were safe, in a way.

Lulu went downstairs and left this note on the kitchen table:

Dear Grammie or Bertie (whoever comes home first),

I had to go to practice. It is at Hart Crane Middle School. Bertie, please come pick up JeDatsun A.S.A.P.

Love,

Lulu

P.S. I will use Spic 'n' Span on the bathroom wall as soon as I get back.

Chapter 17

It was the hottest time of the day. Lulu had always ridden her bike, never walked, from Grammie's to Hart Crane field, and she definitely had never made the trip carrying a baby.

Jenny, scooped up from the bathroom floor, stayed fast asleep in her arms. Her face looked like a rainbow. Lulu hadn't wanted to take a chance on washing it and waking her up. Her head rolled around on Lulu's shoulder, and her pink sneakers bumped against Lulu's thigh. Lulu wiped her brow and wished she had her cap back to shade her eyes. There was, she began to notice, a bad smell in the air. Jenny felt like a twenty-five-pound sack of peaches.

Lulu passed the Dairy Dell and knew she was half-way there. Carrying this weight would be good for her batting muscles. Wrinkling her nose against the rising stink, whatever it was, Lulu trudged down the hill.

Then, just as the field came into sight, she had a terrible thought. A very terrible thought. Gently lifting Jenny away from her chest she saw, smack in the middle of her T-shirt, a dark wet spot.

Oh, no! How could she have forgotten? How could she have been so lamebrained? Diapers! Babies wore diapers, and more important than that, diapers had to be changed! How could she have been so absent-minded? And how was she supposed to play ball in a shirt reeking of baby pee?

She'd have to go back to Grammie's. She couldn't play ball—again. Lulu looked longingly across the grass to the neat, packed base paths and the heavy, patient bases. Jenny hung around her neck like a boulder. Her soppy diaper claimed Lulu like a branding iron.

She bit the insides of her cheeks to keep the tears back, a trick she'd taught herself in kindergarten when she'd been scared of kids bigger than she was. But as she turned back toward Grammie's, a car beeped. It was Coach Angell.

"Lulu! I was hoping you'd make it today!" He leaned out his window. "That's our girl! Way to go!"

"Thanks, coach."

"That's not the little girl, is it?"

"Huh? Oh, you mean Datsun here? This is just a little girl I'm baby-sitting. I have a job baby-sitting her, and her mother is late, and—"

"Come on. I want all the guys to congratulate you."

Coach Angell had the team give three cheers for Lulu. Her ears burning, she clasped Jenny tight against her chest to cover the wet spot. But the cheers finally woke the baby. Immediately, she began to squirm and kick, wanting to get down and mess with the equipment. Lulu's teammates pounded her on the back and socked her in the shoulder till she felt as if she'd gone ten rounds with Sylvester Stallone.

"Great catch, Lu."

"My grandmother read about you way down in Florida. She called me up to ask if I knew you. I said, 'I sure do!' "

"My mom said you're gonna be on TV. Are you really?"

But several of her teammates eyed her and Jenny suspiciously. Were they wondering how a nothing like her had managed to turn into a hero overnight? Did they think she'd pulled a fast one on everybody? Or was it the rising ammonia fumes they were wondering about? Jenny's rainbow complexion? Or what in the world Lulu thought she was doing showing up for practice with this little greased pig of a baby in her arms?

"It'd be nice if she'd make some great catches like

that around here," said one, and a few others laughed. Lulu's ears got hotter.

"They're just jealous," said the girl whose grandmother lived in Florida. "They wish they were heroes too."

"But I'm not really a he—"

Then a pebble hit Lulu on the earlobe.

At first she thought Jenny had bitten her. But then it happened again, and this time she saw the little stone as it whizzed by her nose. Turning around, she spotted a pink bean pole skulking behind a distant backstop.

"Mamamamamama!" Jenny made a crash landing and started to run. Lulu threw her arms across the wet spot. Everyone turned to see Tilda, who began flapping both bony arms as Jenny ran toward her. Jenny shinnied up her mother like Jack up the beanstalk. Everyone turned to stare at Lulu.

"Um, er—I'll be right back," she said, and sprinted across the grass.

Tilda was bending over a big shopping bag. She pulled out a beautiful bride doll and handed it to Jenny, who gave a whoop of pleasure and crushed it to her chest.

"You found a job!" cried Lulu. They were saved! Only someone who had a job—a really good job—could buy an expensive doll like that. "I knew you'd do it! I knew you'd get something great on your first try. What's the job? When do you start?"

Tilda looked up. Fog rolled in over the long gray eyes.

"I missed Jenny so much, when I saw that doll I just couldn't—you know. Resist."

Lulu screeched to a halt. "But what's your job?"

Tilda shook her head.

"What do you mean, no?"

"No job!" said Tilda. "What do you think I mean?"

"No job? You didn't find a job, and you bought that doll?"

Tilda nodded.

"But—but a doll like that must've taken all the rest of your money!"

"It sure did," said Tilda. She turned away and flung an arm up over her face.

"No, Mama! No cry!" said Jenny. She bit her mother on the knee. Tilda gave a yelp. Jenny threw her doll on the ground and kicked it.

Lulu slowly crossed her arms over the wet spot. Head down, she tramped back across the field.

"I'm sorry, coach, but I can't make practice. My job's not over yet."

Chapter 18

Tilda changed Jenny with a spare diaper from her purse. Then, as they walked back to Grammie's, she told her story.

"I took the bus downtown. I was never in a real city before. I was lost for a long time till I finally asked a cop to give me—you know. Directions. I went to one of those jobs in the paper. It was in an office building with two whole walls of elevators and fountains and plants and these gigantic paintings of zippers. Everybody had a briefcase and a suit on, and they looked like somebody had wound them up and set them going. They all knew exactly where they were going in that big place. Everybody except—you know. Me."

Lulu pictured Tilda, in her pink dress and electric blue eyelids, the enormous purse with the photo of Jenny inside slung from her shoulder, wandering up and down the carpeted hallways. With a small shock, she realized that Tilda must have been completely out of place.

"I had to go up to the twelfth floor. That elevator was like a rocket. I felt like I had left half myself down below. Finally I found the personnel. That's where you apply, the personnel. The lady at the desk looked at me like I was something the cat forgot to bury. 'Do you have experience as a receptionist?' she said in this real snotty voice. She was about five feet tall—practically a midget. I could've creamed her with one hand behind my back. I was all ready to tell this big story I'd made up about all the places I'd worked, but somehow it got stuck in my throat. I said, 'The only job I ever had was selling tickets at the town pool.' She said, 'This job is for an experienced receptionist. I'm sorry.' Before she even finished saying it, she was turning back to her computer. If she was sorry, I'm Miss Ohio!"

By now Tilda had stopped crying, but her face was a mess. Her makeup was slipping and sliding all over the place, and a few wisps of hair had gotten stuck in it. She hardly looked like Tilda at all. Jenny, in her arms, was hugging the bride doll and being very quiet.

"Then what did you do?"

"Then? Then I went and sat in Public Square with the old men and the pigeons."

"Then what?"

"Then I got on the bus and came home. No, first I saw the bride doll in a window and bought it, and then I came home."

"You mean you didn't apply anyplace else? You just sat in the square the whole rest of the day?"

Tilda drooped. She drooped so badly, it was as if she'd had her spine removed. "That's right," she said.

"I can't believe it."

"Believe it."

"But how come?"

Tilda sent a pebble flying with her toe. "When that snot turned me down, I knew it was no use," she said. "It's just like my mother always said. I know where *my* nose points, all right. To the nearest disaster."

Lulu looked at Tilda's nose, which was long and sharp and shiny from her tears. How could she have let one midget woman deflate her like that? Tilda, the desperado, the robber queen? Tilda, whose husband sent her daily love letters from halfway around the world? Tilda, the giant who defied her mother, who wore more makeup than anyone Lulu had ever met, and who claimed her fastball had been clocked at sixty-eight miles per hour at the Geauga County Fair?

"Riding back here on the bus, I knew—you know. I was letting you down. I knew you were counting on me finding something. Don't think that didn't make me feel even more rotten. But it's about time you knew the truth, Lulu. You're involved with a—you know."

"What?"

"A failure."

Lulu saw that Tilda was about to start crying all over again. Jenny saw it, too, and bit her mother on the ear.

"Ouch! Jenny!"

"She doesn't like you to cry."

"I never do." And Tilda's forehead began to pucker again, just the way Jenny's did before she let out a wail. "I thought I could start new here. I thought once I got away from my mother and all that junk, things would be different. But it's just like she said. I mess everything up. I'm just a screw-up, that's all."

Lulu was astonished. "Just because you got turned down once?"

"It would've been the same if I went to a hundred places. Nobody'll want me."

"But—but you're so strong! You're so pretty! You're—you're like an electrical storm or something."

"Shoot, are you ever wrong." By now her chin was almost on a level with Lulu's forehead.

"You mean—you're a fake?" asked Lulu.

"That's as good a way to put it as any."

"Gammie!" said Jenny. They'd come to Grammie's house by now, and Jenny stretched her arms toward it. Tilda took a swipe at her bleary eyes.

"How am I going to tell her I didn't find anything and I'm broke?"

"Just tell her."

"I can't live off charity. Tomorrow we'll have to go."

"Where?"

Tilda didn't bother to answer. But at the front steps she stopped.

"You know what I really wish right now? That I was playing ball. It used to be, when I felt rottenest, that was the only thing could make me feel better." She sounded as if she were describing life back in the Pleistocene Era.

"You sure can throw," said Lulu. "Both those pebbles got me on the ear, and you must've been a hundred feet away."

"See? I was trying for your shoulder. Plus I made you miss practice."

Tilda pushed open the door and took Jenny straight upstairs. When they came back down, she'd repaired her makeup and changed into shorts and a T-shirt. Jenny's face was scrubbed clean. Grammie, who liked to eat early, had a meat loaf (no onions, peppers, or mushrooms) ready. The table was set for four.

"Are you—are you having company for supper?" Tilda asked.

Grammie threw her a look. "Dependable Dan's not company. And since you're living here, neither are you."

"But we're just renting. And I didn't—"

"You'll save me from meat loaf sandwiches all week. I already called your mother, Lulu. Hello, monkey. No need to ask what you've been up to today. I already scrubbed that bathroom, Lulu. Next time I'll leave it to you."

"There won't be a next time, Grammie," said Tilda.

"That's what you think. I know this variety better than you do. Bring the catsup, and I'll tell you about the time Ellie came home from second grade in a squad car."

For the second night in a row, Grammie talked more than Lulu could remember. She cut Jenny's meat into tiny pieces and fed her her peas. Tilda, her head bent, pushed her food around her plate.

"Don't think I'm going to feed you," said Grammie

gruffly, and suddenly Tilda laughed. She lifted her head, and then slowly she began to eat.

After supper, Grammie let Jenny feed Edward the scraps. Then the three of them went into the living room to watch *Wheel of Fortune* while Lulu and Tilda did the dishes.

"You were right," said Tilda. "She didn't even mention me getting a job."

"I think she likes having you here."

"Jenny, anyway."

"You know, there's a couple of old gloves out in the garage. And I never go anywhere without a ball."

They stood in opposite corners of the backyard. Tilda turned the ball in her hands. Even from across the yard, her bony knuckles looked huge pressing against it.

"I feel so rusty," she said. "I feel like the Tin Man before Dorothy found him."

She's trying to get up her courage, thought Lulu. She'd never guessed courage would be something Tilda had to get up. She'd thought it just flowed through her, like sap. But now Lulu thought, *What if she's no good at this either? What if all her bragging about her arm is fake too?*

"Here goes nothing."

Lulu had never caught a meteorite before. The tomatoes should have shriveled from the heat that pitch gave off. Within sixty seconds, Lulu's hand was on fire.

"Did you say you're rusty?"

Tilda grinned. "It's coming back to me."

Grammie, Edward, and Jenny, still dragging her

bride doll, came out just in time to see Lulu leap for a high one and slam against the side of the house. She slithered down into a panting, red-faced heap.

"Go, Mama!" shouted Jenny.

Tilda, not even breathing hard, smiled. "She's my biggest—you know. Fan."

"Where'd you learn to throw like that, Alberta?" Grammie asked.

Tilda pretended to pull a weed from the garden. "Just around."

"You look to me like what they call a natural. Why don't you two go up to the field, where you have more room? Datsun and I are taking Edward for his nightly constitutional."

"Are you sure that's okay? You don't mind taking the baby?"

But Grammie only flipped her hand and gave Jenny the leash. All three of them went at exactly the same speed.

"Take my bike, why don't you?" said Grammie.

So Lulu and Tilda, on Grammie's ancient Schwinn, rode to Hart Crane. They went a roundabout way so they wouldn't have to pass Mrs. Wysocki's. Tilda loped out onto the field, her flyaway hair floating behind her. Her diamonds caught the fierce last light.

Catch is the wrong word for what came next. Lulu had never had a workout like it in her life. Coach Angell never made them work this hard—he was too nice. As soon as he saw anyone getting tired or discouraged, he offered them a drink of ice water and a personal pep talk.

But Tilda didn't even notice when Lulu began to get tired. She didn't seem to notice anything but the ball. She was the best player Lulu had ever seen off the TV screen. Her pitches sizzled. Every one of her long stringy muscles worked in perfect synchronization, pulling the ball down and then putting it exactly where she wanted it. If only that snotty personnel woman could see her now!

Lulu, exhausted, threw another wild one. Tilda loped after it and scolded, "Your catching's not bad, but you've got to work on your arm. Catching the ball's pleasure—knowing what to do with it, that's—you know. Business."

At last, as Lulu scrambled after a grounder that rolled away into the twilight, Tilda smacked her forehead.

"It's getting dark! We left Jenny with Grammie all this time! Come on!"

She grabbed the Schwinn and sped off. But Lulu, whose legs felt like the elastic in ten-year-old underpants, couldn't go that fast, so she had to slow down. Side by side, they rode through the dusky evening streets.

"That was the best practice I ever had in my whole life," said Lulu. "Even if I did miss about seventy-five percent of the balls."

"You weren't bad at all."

"Maybe—maybe you could give me some pointers."

Tilda frowned. "Me?"

"No, the man in the moon up there."

Tilda smiled. "You could have a good arm if you worked on it."

"Me?"

"No, the man in the moon. You'd have to work harder, though. I don't get the feeling you really truly believe you can be good. And beef yourself up! Eat more protein."

"I wish I was tall like you. You have so much power."

Tilda gave a funny smile. "First grade was the first time I realized how big I was. Some girls started making fun of me. They called me Mighty Matilda. After that, I slept with a five-pound sack of rice on my head every night."

"What for?"

"I thought it'd stunt me."

"It didn't work."

"I know."

"There's a girl in my class called Caitlin that everybody likes. She never seems afraid of anything. And everything always works out for her. When I'm eighteen, I might change my name to Caitlin."

"I can't imagine you named anything except Lulu."

Lulu's ears burned. "Really?" she said.

"Except maybe Datsun."

"Well, I can't imagine you short."

They turned down Grammie's street. Jenny, in pajamas printed with bunnies, came running across the lawn. Tilda laid down her bike and swung her baby high over her head.

"I gave her her bath, but she wouldn't go to bed till you got back," said Grammie. "Not that I blame her."

"More! More!" the baby yelled. How she loved to fly! Tilda dipped and swung her. "Look, Datsun!" Jenny cried. "Looka me!"

Tilda's face shone in the dusk, and Jenny's, in orbit, seemed like a reflection of it. *They really love each other,* Lulu thought. *There's no faking that.*

Holding Jenny close, Tilda turned to Lulu.

"Would you—do you think you could baby-sit again tomorrow? So I can go looking again?"

It was a little hard to get the word out over the lump in her throat, but Lulu managed.

"Sure," she said.

Chapter 19

"Hello, stranger."

Lulu's father sat at the kitchen table. He'd cleared a space in the middle of the sandpaper, solvents, and steel wool and was looking at a catalog of bike equipment.

"Hi, Daddy."

"Mom's not back from the library yet. She's researching mildew. Mildew. Bleagh." He stuck out his tongue and crossed his eyes, doing a perfect imitation of Elena. "And you've been helping Grammie with her new roomer."

"Yeah."

"Did you leave your cap there again?"

"I guess so."

"You've got a lot on your mind these days, haven't you?"

Lulu nodded.

"Mom's giving you a hard time about this hero stuff, isn't she?"

Lulu nodded again.

"She's pretty excited about what you did."

"But she's got it all wrong. She thinks I'm different now. But just because one thing happens to you—it doesn't all of a sudden change you!"

"Hm." Her father looked down at his catalog. "You could be right. I don't know many people who've changed much. But . . ." He traced the outline of a wheel with one finger. "But sometimes, well, sometimes, if you're really lucky, something might happen that makes you discover a side of yourself you didn't know you had."

He looked up at Lulu and smiled. "Oh yeah, before I forget. Sissy Potash called you again. She said she called Grammie's and talked to someone very odd. Do you think it could've been that new roomer?" He reached over to the phone pad. "Here's her number."

Sissy Potash! Lulu felt all the strength go out of her.

"Hey, what's that look for?" Her father slipped an arm around her shoulders. "If you don't want to talk to her, just tell her. Call her and tell her you're finished giving interviews."

"But—"

"Mom will be disappointed. That's what you're worried about, right? But she really only wants you to be happy, Lu." He kissed her on the forehead. "I'll talk to Mom. I'll tell her she's got to leave this all up to you. It's all up to you."

If only he knew how right he was.

A few hours later, Lulu awoke to the sound of her parents' voices downstairs. Her mother's skipped up and down like a calliope till her father's, warm and droning, interrupted. Her mother's interrupted back.

Arguing, thought Lulu. *Arguing about me.* She pulled the pillow tight over her ears.

Chapter 20

When Lulu got to Grammie's the next morning, Tilda was already waiting, sitting on the front steps eating a sandwich. She held out half to Lulu.

"Scrambled egg," she said. "Try some."

A scrambled-egg sandwich? Lulu shook her head automatically.

"The only kind of sandwich I eat is peanut butter and jelly."

"I told you, you've gotta build yourself up. Eggs have lots of iron." Tilda thrust the sandwich into Lulu's hand.

She took the tiniest bite possible. The bread was soft. The egg was creamy. No onions and no lumps. There was a generous shot of catsup.

"It's good," Lulu said in amazement.

"You think I'd give you something rotten?"

Just then, the paper boy tossed the morning paper at them. Tilda pulled out the want ads, looked at them as if they were rat poison, and marched off down the street.

Lulu watched her go. *Should I have told her her mother and Sissy Potash are hot on her trail?* she wondered. *But what good would it do? It would only make her more upset. And today she needs all the confidence she can find.*

Grammie stayed home today, so taking care of Jenny was easier. The three of them poked in the garden while Edward lay panting in the shade of the plum tree. Lulu pushed Jenny in the stroller to the store for milk. After lunch, Grammie announced she was taking a siesta and Jenny could sleep with her in her big bed. Lulu expected a five-star tantrum, but instead Jenny took Grammie's hand and the two of them climbed the stairs. When Lulu looked in on them twenty minutes later, Jenny, her thumb in her mouth and her cap on her head, was curled in a ball against Grammie's stomach. Both of them were snoring.

Lulu wandered around the house and yard. The Indians were off today, and she didn't have any practice. She tried not to think about Tilda being turned down by snotty people in business suits. She tried to think of a job she could help Tilda get. With one of her mother's friends, maybe? But Elena's friends were things like midwives and weavers and auto mechanics—jobs Tilda did not seem qualified for. Lulu got her glove and ball and went out on the front lawn to play catch with herself. If only David could hire her—but he couldn't afford an assistant. Every few minutes, Lulu went to the curb and looked up the street for Tilda.

Each time a car slowed, her heart skipped a beat. Was it Tilda's mother? Had Sissy Potash finally put two and two together and figured out where she was?

Lulu was on the back steps husking corn for supper and trying to keep Jenny from eating the silk when the back door opened.

"Mama!"

Tilda scooped up the baby as if she weighed about as much as a first-class letter. But there wasn't any doll today. And there wasn't, Lulu saw from one look at her face, any job either.

"I started off going to those big places again. But I just got the same treatment. One place took my application, but they probably threw it out the minute I was out the door."

"They can't do that!"

"So then I decided I'd better go somewhere that wasn't so fancy. So I went to Woolworth's and Pay Less Shoes and someplace called The Nut House, even though the smell of nuts roasting makes me sick. Nothing. Nobody wanted me."

"Want me," said Jenny, nestling against her mother.

"Maybe I'm too tall. Maybe I dress wrong, or talk wrong, or smell wrong. Maybe I have BO or bad breath and nobody ever told me."

"You're doing the best you can! Everybody strikes out sometimes! Every pitcher gives up a homer!"

"And plenty of guys get sent back to the farm."

That night, Grammie served wieners and beans. She told about the time Elena poured cooking oil all up and down the hallway so she could "ice skate." She talked so much, it was easy not to notice how quiet Tilda was.

While they washed the dishes, Lulu tried to think of

the best way to tell Tilda about her mother. Finally she said, "Want to go have a catch?"

A light shone in Tilda's pale, stormy face. But she said, "I'm through with baseball. Baseball's kid stuff."

"Baseball?"

"I have to find a job. I don't have time for games."

But she was already drying her hands. "I'm just doing this for you. For all you've—you know. Done for me. I'm through with baseball myself."

Tonight they took Jenny and a bat with them. After fielding grounders for a while, Tilda asked Lulu to show her her stance.

"Tighten up. Not that much! A hair's breadth. All right. Now, bend your knees a little more."

"This feels awful. I couldn't hit a basketball standing like this!"

"You're just not used to it. All right, eye on the ball."

Lulu fanned one pitch after another.

"I told you!" she said. "Let me do it my old way."

But Tilda held up a hand. "You're trying too hard. Loosen up. Take it easy."

"I can't."

"Believe me. You've got to trust yourself."

Lulu slammed the next pitch over Tilda's head. Tilda nodded solemnly.

"What did I tell you?" she said.

"It was just an accident!" cried Lulu, trying not to roll on the ground with pleasure.

Tilda shook her head slowly. "There are no accidents."

That was when the magic started to work on them. That night, it seemed as if they could play forever. One more catch, one more swing, their muscles working and their nerves tingling. Twilight knit up the corners of the field, the smell of the neighborhood barbecues faded, and still they played. Even when her throw went wild or her glove closed on nothing, Lulu knew what her error had been and couldn't wait to try again.

The magic was in Tilda too. She was all over the field, arms and legs like the blades of some miraculous machine. Once she showed Lulu how to slide, sending up a cloud of dust like a human twister. Jenny ran and threw herself on top of her, shouting for joy.

Finally, as she was sprinting toward left field, Lulu's legs gave out. She fell forward, then rolled over and lay on her back, trying to catch her breath. The sun was gone, on its way to the other side of the world. A few dark thin clouds trailed across the dusk, making Lulu remember that bird she'd seen at dawn, the one with the skinny legs.

"Are you okay?" Tilda suddenly loomed over her.

Just then Jenny, that other bird, came skimming over the grass and threw herself across Lulu's stomach.

"Oof!"

"Datsun!"

"Say Lulu," Tilda told her. "Lu-lu!"

"Datsun."

"That's okay," said Lulu. "I'm getting to like Datsun. It makes me feel like I have a secret identity."

Tilda plucked a few blades of grass. Her diamonds

sparkled in the dusk. Down at the end of her long skinny legs, her hightops loomed up in the grass like loaves of bread. The air smelled of fresh-cut grass, and a passing car's radio played a happy, toe-tapping song. When Tilda spoke, she said exactly what Lulu was thinking.

"I wish we could stay here forever."

"Me too."

"But we can't."

Now was the time. Lulu sat up, tumbling Jenny off her. "Tilda, I've got some bad news."

Tilda froze. She made a little choking sound. "My mother?"

Lulu told her about the calls from Sissy Potash.

"And you didn't tell me all this time?"

"I didn't want to get you upset. Once you told me how hard looking for a job was, I—"

Lulu saw Tilda's face begin to blur. It was just like that very first day, when she'd opened her apartment door to see Mrs. Wysocki standing there holding Jenny. Tilda was trying to disappear. And now Lulu knew it really was because she was so scared.

"What about your husband?" Lulu cried. "Can't we send him a telegram or something? Maybe he could send you some money special delivery. I bet he could! He loves you. He'll save you!"

But now Tilda made a sound like gargling, or a stream thawing in the spring. "He can't."

"But how come? What kind of husband is he?"

"He's invisible, that's what."

"Huh?"

"Oh, Lulu." Tilda tore up a fistful of grass and threw it down. "I don't have any husband. I made the whole story up."

Very slowly, Lulu lay back down in the grass. Her ears began to burn.

"Oh," she said.

"I lied. I told you, I'm a failure. First string. I don't blame you if you're mad. You've got every right."

"Oh," Lulu said again.

"Oh oh," said Jenny.

"I've been lying to you all along. Nobody loves me from halfway around the world. Nobody loves me at all, except Jenny. It's just—you know. The two of us."

Lulu stared up at the sky, where the first star twinkled. Like a diamond in the sky.

"I always thought your husband gave you those diamond earrings," she said.

"Ha. I bought them myself. And they're not real diamonds."

"Oh."

After a minute, Lulu heard Tilda stand up. She heard Jenny call, "Datsun!" and Tilda softly say, "Hush!"

Then she heard the enormous hightops trudge away across the field.

Chapter 21

Lulu rode home slowly. The streets were quiet. The moon was rising. It wasn't quite full, and it looked wobbly, as if it might just roll away out of sight.

"Lambchop! Where have you been?" Her mother came running down from the front porch.

"Didn't Grammie tell you?"

"You can't play ball in the dark! We were so worried about you! Daddy's out right now, riding around looking for you."

"Sorry." Lulu wheeled her bike toward the garage, and her mother followed.

"I should be mad at you! If you weren't so good all the time, I would be. Instead, I was just scared to death."

Elena grabbed Lulu in a rib-cracking hug. Lulu's nose mashed against her T-shirt, which smelled of spackling compound and Ivory soap.

"Who's this crazy roomer you were playing with? I can't believe my mother, letting you go off with a stranger like that! She's always been so cautious. She's always been so cautious, she drives me bananas. What's gotten into her? And what's gotten into *you?* Leaving the house at dawn, staying out till nearly dark, missing a game—Mr. Angell told me. He called today. He said you missed a practice too. He said, 'I was just wondering, is anything wrong with Lulu? She doesn't seem herself.' I told him, 'This hero stuff has thrown her for a real loop.' "

"That's right," Lulu said into her mother's T-shirt. "A real loop."

"I said, 'She's like a different person.' "

"That should make you happy," said Lulu into the shirt.

"What?" Elena lifted Lulu's chin.

"Nothing."

"Lulu, have you been crying?"

"No!"

"Your eyes are all red."

"Like you said, I've been up since dawn."

"Isn't there something you want to tell me?"

Lulu looked into her mother's eyes, which were suddenly brimming.

"You've been like a stranger these past couple of days, Lulu. I missed you. I missed you a lot."

Nobody missed Tilda. Nobody loved her, except crazy little Jenny. At that moment, Lulu knew how lucky she was. Luck seemed to fold itself around her like a pair of golden wings.

"Mom—" she said.

But her mother didn't wait for her to go on. "The *Sun Press* came out today, and you're on the front page of that too. The phone started ringing again, and then that

With a Name Like Lulu, Who Needs More Trouble?

Sissy Potash called again, and I was so tired of hearing her snippy, pushy voice, and I was missing you so much and so mad at you for staying away and being so stubborn and not talking to her and not telling me what was going on, I told her, sure. Come tomorrow at nine-thirty, and Lulu will give you an interview."

Lulu jumped out of her mother's arms. The golden wings dissolved.

"You what?"

"She just wants to interview you! Not boil you in oil!"

"You didn't have any right to tell her that! It's up to me!"

"You should be proud of yourself, Lulu! Instead, you act like you've got something to hide!"

"It's my business! Why do you always have to try and run everything? Why can't you just leave me alone?"

Elena stood very still. "Leave you alone? I'm your mother."

"You're the one who's always talking about how important feelings are. So how come you can't just let me have my own feelings? How come you have to take over?"

"How come you never talk to me? How come you keep everything to yourself? Don't you know how that makes me feel? I hardly ever know what's going on inside you."

"Maybe if you didn't ask so much, I'd tell you."

"That's crazy, Lulu."

"Maybe there's things you wouldn't understand."

"I'd try."

"No, you wouldn't. You'd just tell me I should be different from how I am."

"Lambchop, the only reason I want you to be on that TV show, or to let Potash interview you, is because you did something extraordinary. And I want you to be as proud as I am."

"You can't just order somebody to be proud of themselves."

Elena paused again. "You're right," she said.

"So call Sissy Potash back and tell her not to come tomorrow."

"No way, Lulu. If you don't want to talk to her, you tell her. *You* explain to her. I can't! I can't explain the first thing about you, Lulu Leone Duckworth-Greene!"

With that Elena turned on her bare heel and stalked back into the house.

Chapter 22

Lulu lay in bed, but she didn't sleep. Her parents had long ago come up to their room, but she still hadn't closed her eyes. Moonlight streamed through the window, past the crooked curtains, and hit her fortune, hanging on the wall: HIDDEN RESOURCES ARE AT YOUR COMMAND.

After a very long time she got up, pulled on her jeans and T-shirt, and tiptoed downstairs. In spite of the moon, it seemed very black outside. The air was cool and damp and smelled of things that come out in the dark. As Lulu slipped into the garage, she saw a robber crouching there! No, it was a bale of peat moss. Gritting her teeth, she groped her way to her bike. The iciness of the handlebars sent a shiver through her.

The streets were empty. The houses were dark. Lulu imagined that car up at the intersection slowly turning and coming toward her. She began to plan what she would do if it drew up beside her and the horrible person inside stuck out his horrible, long-toothed head. But the car, with two teenagers sitting very close together, glided quickly by.

At Grammie's house, she gathered a handful of pebbles. It was a good thing Edward was deaf and Grammie snored. Her aim was perfect. Tilda appeared at her window instantly, then disappeared.

The side door opened soundlessly, and Tilda stood there in the moonlight. She wore a red-and-white-striped nightshirt that made her look like a walking candy cane. In the dark without her makeup, she looked so young, she might almost have passed for one of Lulu's classmates.

"Sissy Potash is coming to my house in the morning to

interview me. There's no way I can get out of it this time."

"You came here in the middle of the night to tell me that?"

"Yeah."

"How come? I thought you were through with us. I thought you—you know. Washed your hands."

"You lied to me, Tilda."

"Sure I lied. I knew if I told the truth, you wouldn't want to have anything to do with me. And that's just what happened." She took a step forward. Her fine hair was full of knots, as if she'd done a lot of tossing and turning. "Except now you're here."

"You shouldn't've lied to me."

"You rode all the way over here alone? I thought you told me you were afraid of the dark."

"I am."

"It's pretty dark."

"I guess—I guess I'm more afraid of other stuff."

Tilda took another step forward. Moonlight lay like slivers of mirror on her shoulders.

"Like what?" she asked.

"Like—how could you lie to me all that time? I thought we were—you know."

"No, I don't know."

"Yes, you do."

Tilda bent so her face was level with Lulu's. Her eyes were like lakes in the moonlight. "All this time, you've only been helping me because you thought it was the right thing to do, right?"

"Wrong."

"Then why?"

Lulu looked down. In the moonlight Tilda's bare feet glowed like great slabs of mother of pearl. Tilda had been able to say "I'm a robber." But not "Nobody loves me."

"Ever since I met you, Tilda, it's like I'm a different person."

Tilda grabbed Lulu's shoulder in that familiar, painful iron grip.

"You're not through with us? Even though you know everything about us? Even that it's just the two of us?"

Lulu looked at Tilda's big toe.

"I thought it was the three of us," she said.

Tilda let go of Lulu's shoulder. Then, slowly, she reached back out and gently rubbed it.

"Is it just the moonlight? Or are your ears really that red?"

"I don't usually spill my guts like that."

"You should. You've got the best guts of anybody I ever met."

Chapter 23

"The best guts of anybody I ever met." Tilda's eyes narrowed. "And you're going to need them now."

They walked out back by the garden, to make sure they didn't wake Grammie or Jenny.

"First thing in the morning, I'll call Sissy Potash," Lulu said. "I'll tell her you just got a letter that a long-lost aunt in—in England died, and you inherited all her money. You and Jenny caught the first flight over, and now you live on an estate where Jenny has a nanny and her own pony."

"You're the worst liar I ever met," said Tilda, "and I've met plenty. Nobody's going to believe that!"

"Then I'll say—"

"You won't have to say anything, because I'm going to be right there with you."

"But you can't!"

"You've done enough sneaking around for me. I don't want you doing any more."

"I don't mind sneaking around for you."

"I mind. I told you a lie, and I almost lost you for a friend. I'll tell them you're innocent. I'll tell them you were just trying to do the right thing. You'd better get home now, before your parents find out you're gone."

The next morning, when Lulu came downstairs, she hardly recognized the house. Everything was cleaned up. All the tools and sandpaper and chemicals were put away, and there were jars of peonies and roses everywhere. The air smelled of fresh-squeezed lemons and baking muffins.

"Morning, Lu!" Elena had pinned her hair into a motherly bun. "Ready for the execution? The firing squad should be here in about ten minutes." She smiled, showing her crooked tooth. "I'm sorry, lambchop. It's going to be okay. Trust me! You might even wind up enjoying somebody telling you how wonderful you are!"

David had closed his shop for the morning and was wearing the button-down shirt Grammie had given him for Christmas. He was looking for a scissors to snip off the tag.

"It'll be over before you know it," he told Lulu. He glanced out the window. "Yikes, she's here already! She must really be hyper to meet you, Lu. But who's that with her?"

Elena ran to the window and groaned. "It's that Mrs. Wysocki! Poor Lulu will be lucky if she gets a word in edgewise!"

Mrs. Wysocki wore a dress like a purple tent and sunglasses with rhinestones. When she saw Lulu, she clapped her on the head so hard, Lulu was surprised it didn't sink between her shoulders.

"There's my girl!" Mrs. Wysocki cried. "How are you, dearie? Surprised to see me?"

"Mrs. Wysocki insisted on coming," said Sissy Potash. She smiled hard at Lulu. Her mouth seemed to have extra teeth. She was dressed all in black, except for pointy purple boots. "She was afraid you'd be too modest to tell your story, Lulu. Even though I assured her you were looking forward to talking to me."

I never said that.

David gave Mrs. Wysocki and Sissy Potash the two armchairs, and he and Elena took the love seat. That left Lulu the kitchen chair, the one with the rungs that dug into your back.

But where's Tilda?

Sissy Potash set a tape recorder next to the basket of muffins.

"I know this won't bother you," she said, giving it an affectionate little pat. "Just pretend it's not there."

The chair bit into Lulu's back. The room seemed to be growing hotter by the second.

Mrs. Wysocki helped herself to a muffin. "Don't worry," she said. She still had her sunglasses on, as if she were a famous celebrity. "If Lulu forgets anything, I'll fill you right in, Mrs. Potash."

Sissy Potash didn't take her eyes off Lulu. She smiled exactly like a nurse trying to distract you before she jabs you with a needle.

"All right then," she said. "The beginning's always a good place to start. On the day of the rescue, you were on your way to play baseball. You must be a superb player, Lulu, to have made a catch like that! You must have been completely confident of your ability!"

Lulu ran a finger around the neck of her T-shirt. "It didn't feel like I caught her. It felt like someone else did."

Sissy Potash had a jangly laugh. "But it *was* you, wasn't it, Lulu?"

"It sure was!" said Mrs. Wysocki, wiping her mouth with a napkin. "There I was, just getting dressed, when a little voice came over my speaker. Timid as a mouse! 'I have a little lost girl—'"

"Of course it was Lulu!" said Elena, cutting Mrs. Wysocki off. "David always said she'd surprise us someday."

Sissy Potash took the lemonade Elena was handing her. She settled back into her armchair, and now Lulu thought of a black widow getting cozy in her web.

"I'll tell you what. Let's give Lulu a chance to tell her own story. Go ahead."

Elena sat on the edge of the love seat. Her hair was already breaking loose from its bun. Beside her, David nodded at Lulu and sent her his most encouraging smile.

Lulu cleared her throat. It felt as if half a peanut butter sandwich (chunky style) had gotten stuck in it. Her ears already felt like twin torches.

Where's Tilda?

"First I helped Grammie in her garden," she began. She told what she and Grammie had planted that day, and what they'd had for lunch. She even described the

Indians game and how they'd been ahead when she left. She put in as many details as she possibly could, including Willie Upshaw's spectacular double in the bottom of the second. She tried to drag out this part of the story as long as possible.

Where was Tilda? Had she changed her mind? Was she going to leave it all up to Lulu after all—again? Did she want Lulu to cover up for her—again? Lulu saw her mother begin to tap her foot, Mrs. Wysocki reach for another muffin, and Sissy Potash's smile grow thin.

Finally, she couldn't drag it out anymore. She had to tell the part about looking up and seeing Jenny in the window.

"She was pushing on the screen. I saw one corner of it was frayed, so—"

Sissy Potash sat forward so abruptly, lemonade splashed onto her pointy purple toes. "Frayed? The screen was frayed?"

Now Mrs. Wysocki bolted upright. Muffin crumbs flew. "I didn't know that! She never told me!"

"The screen was obviously in disrepair, Lulu?" asked Sissy Potash.

"I didn't know that!" protested Mrs. Wysocki. "That's the kind of tenant Tilda Hubbard was. Never said a word to me. The ceiling could've fallen on her head, and she wouldn't've said boo. If I'd known that screen was broken, I would've had it fixed pronto."

"It sounds as if the tear was clearly visible. Isn't that what you said, Lulu? You could see the hole from the sidewalk?"

"It wasn't exactly a hole. It was—"

"The screen needed to be repaired. Isn't that what you said?"

"I guess so."

Sissy Potash tapped her tape recorder as if to tell it, "Be sure and get that." Mrs. Wysocki wiped her brow with a napkin.

"It'll be fixed tomorrow, I guarantee."

"Let's hope so," said Sissy Potash sternly.

As Mrs. Wysocki fanned herself with a napkin, Lulu went on.

"Well, so I shouted at her not to do it, but she just laughed. That's the kind of baby she is. When you tell her not to do something, that's all she wants to do. What happened was, she didn't fall. She jumped."

Lulu paused a moment, hoping they would see the difference. But they all just stared at her, waiting for her to continue.

"The screen tore, and she jumped. And I caught her." She held out her arms.

"And how did you feel at that moment?"

"Huh?"

Sissy Potash jackknifed toward her. "How did it feel to hold that baby in your arms? To know you'd saved her from serious injury, perhaps even death? What were your thoughts at that moment, Lulu Leone?"

"I thought, 'Whew! I'm glad that's over.'"

Elena threw back her head and laughed. David chuckled. Mrs. Wysocki took off her sunglasses and looked hopeful that she'd been forgiven.

TRICIA SPRINGSTUBB

But Sissy Potash wasn't sidetracked. She was holding her lemonade in both hands, and an ice cube popped. The room grew hotter yet, and to Lulu, Sissy Potash seemed to swell like a balloon in the Macy's Thanksgiving Day parade.

The chair rungs dug deeper into her back, and she began to sweat. Where was Tilda? Had she given into that awful, blurry, flatten-out-like-a-pancake fear? Had she run away again?

"Was that *all* you thought?" asked Sissy Potash.

"I figured I better get her back to her mother."

"Her mother," said Sissy Potash. "Yes. I'm very interested in this part of the story." She tapped her tape recorder, which seemed instantly to grow larger too. "You brought the baby up to her apartment. The mother opened the door, and when Mrs. Wysocki told her what had happened, she slammed the door in your faces."

"Weird," said Elena.

"Right," said Sissy Potash. She was on the very edge of her seat. "Then she changed her mind, opened the door, and pulled you inside." Sissy Potash swelled to mammoth proportions. "Lulu, what did she say when the two of you were alone? How did she act? What kind of person was Matilda Hubbard?"

"She . . . she . . ."

"Only you know what she had to say for herself that day. Believe me, how you answer is much more important than you realize. How did she express her remorse? Her gratitude? Did she cry? Did she hug you?

Tell us, Lulu—*what kind of person is Matilda Hub-bard?*"

"She's just a regular person! Just like me! She's good at some things and not good at other things, that's all! She's just a person!"

Sissy Potash touched her tape recorder, zeroing in for the kill. "You sound as if you know her very well."

"I do! I mean, I do? I mean—"

"Datsun!"

Jenny came first, as usual. Then Tilda stood in the living-room doorway. She wore her one and only dress and her hightops. Though she was pale as spaghetti, she stood very straight.

"I'm Matilda Hubbard. I understand you people have some—you know. Questions."

Chapter 24

David brought in another kitchen chair, and Tilda sat down next to Lulu.

"It took a lot longer than I thought to walk here," she told Lulu quietly. "Especially with Jenny screaming 'Want out!' the whole way."

Sissy Potash carefully set her lemonade down.

"Ms. Hubbard," she said, "this *is* a surprise. We thought you'd left town."

"That's what I wanted you to think."

Sissy Potash crossed and uncrossed her legs. She tapped her tape recorder. "You're saying you deliberately misled us?"

"That's right."

"The obvious question is, Why?"

"So I could hide out."

"Datsun!" Jenny scrambled into Lulu's lap. Lulu had never seen her so dressed up. Not only was she wearing a neatly ironed party dress, but her hair was in two smooth braids. Even the baseball cap looked cleaner. Grammie must have done it. Jenny would never have sat still long enough for anyone else.

"Datsun!" Jenny swung her feet into her mother's lap so that she made a little bridge between them. Sissy Potash, alert as a bloodhound, watched.

"So you could hide out," she repeated. "Once again I have to ask you, Why?"

"I needed some—you know. Time."

"I'm confused, Ms. Hubbard. Could you be a little more concise?"

"Give her a chance!" Lulu cried. Suddenly, Jenny was like a wire, conducting courage into her. "She'll tell you! That's why she's here!"

"It's okay, Lulu," said Tilda. Holding on to Jenny's shoes, she looked directly at Sissy Potash. "It was my fault she fell out that window."

"She jumped!" cried Lulu.

"Yumped!" agreed Jenny.

Tilda didn't take her eyes off Sissy Potash. "Fell or jumped, it was my fault. I—I haven't done that great a job of being a mother."

"It's hard work! I didn't know how hard it was till I started taking care of Jenny."

"Yenny!"

Sissy Potash drew a hand down the side of her face. "Taking care of Jenny?" she repeated.

"Yenny!"

"I'm looking for a job, Ms. Potash. I'm looking as hard as I know how. Lulu takes care of Jenny while I do it. I'd have—you know. Croaked by now, if it wasn't for Lulu. She's missed practice and everything for me. She could get kicked off the team for missing. You probably don't know the first thing about baseball, do you, so you don't know what that means. Jenny and I have—you know. Wrecked her entire life."

"That's not true!" cried Lulu. "That is one hundred percent wrong! Besides, you should see Tilda's change-up! She can even throw a knuckler sometimes, if the wind's right. She—"

"If you're still in town," broke in Mrs. Wysocki, "where have you been living? Where'd you and that little lamb go when you folded up your tent and stole away in the night?"

"And if you don't have a job," added Sissy Potash, "may I ask what you're living on?"

Tilda stared down at her hightops. The room was

absolutely still. Lulu knew Sissy Potash was waiting for The Confession. She was waiting for Tilda to say, "On my mother's stolen money."

Instead Tilda whispered, "You know. Kindness."

"May I ask whose?"

Tilda raised her head. "I'll only tell you on one—you know. Condition. You have to swear you won't bother her. She's completely innocent. She doesn't know who I am."

"That's right," said Lulu. "Grammie thinks her name is Alberta Watson!"

"Grammie?" Elena's voice was a whisper. *"Grammie?"*

"I had to do it, Mom! Tilda didn't have anyplace to go! She didn't have any money or any friends or any—" *Any husband.* "She didn't have anything, and I had to save her from her mother."

Elena shook her head slowly, and her bun went completely to pieces. "Save her from her *mother*?"

Sissy Potash held up a hand. "Let me see if I can get this straight. Lulu, you helped Ms. Hubbard sneak out of Mrs. Wysocki's building and into your grandmother's, where she's been living in secret all this time?"

Tilda jumped up, flinging Jenny's feet out of her lap. "That's right. And if you hold that against Lulu or Grammie, I'll . . . I'll . . ."

"Who's talking about me behind my back?"

When Jenny saw Grammie in the living-room doorway, she jumped off Lulu's lap and ran toward her, bumping the table and knocking a glass of lemonade onto Sissy Potash's purple boots. Sissy jumped up, too, and stepped on Jenny's toes. Jenny whirled around and bit her on the knee.

"Hey! Yow!" yelled Sissy Potash.

"Tsk tsk, now you know why I never visit here, Ellie," said Grammie. "There's no peace for a minute. Hello, monkey." She nodded to Sissy Potash. "I was talking to the baby there, not you."

Sissy Potash swabbed her boot with a napkin. When she stood back up to face Grammie's glare, she tottered.

"Another surprise visitor. This certainly is turning out to be an—an interesting morning."

"My daughter here specializes in surprises."

"It's your granddaughter who's providing most of the surprises today, Mrs. —"

"Is that so." Grammie looked at Lulu. "Bertie told me you were getting interviewed."

"Mrs. . . . Grammie, I have some news that will shock you. This is the young woman whose baby Lulu saved. She's been living with you under false pretenses."

"Is that a fact." Grammie looked down at Jenny. "So her name's not Datsun?"

"Her name is Jennifer Hubbard."

"Huh. I was just getting used to Datsun."

"Mrs. . . . Grammie, you don't understand. Tilda and your granddaughter have—"

"I understand all right," Grammie said with such cool dignity, Lulu felt a little shock. Could Grammie have known all along? "I'm not senile, you know."

"But they tricked you!"

"Names don't mean much to me. Bertie's a lovely girl. She's been a great help to me, fixing things around the house I don't like to bother Ellie and David for. Her baby's a little bit out of hand, but she's coming along, aren't you, monkey? No, I don't have any complaints. Ask my daughter. No one is fussier about who she shares her house with than I am. Isn't that right, El?"

Like a vase so full that any movement would make it spill, Lulu's mother rose slowly to her feet. "That's right, Mom."

"Yoos! Yoos for Yenny!" Jenny made a sudden lunge for the lemonade pitcher, but Lulu intercepted. She poured an inch into a cup and helped Jenny drink. When it dribbled onto the baby's chin, she wiped it off. Looking up, Lulu saw her mother standing perfectly still, transfixed.

"I'm glad you're not upset, Mrs. . . . Grammie, but I'm afraid you will be when you know the whole story. Lulu, I know you had the best intentions. First you saved the baby, and then you tried to save the mother too."

"Tilda doesn't need any saving!" cried Lulu. "She just needs a chance."

Jenny suddenly began to cry. Grammie picked her up. "Too much excitement, even for the monkey," she said, and gave Sissy Potash what could only be called a dirty look.

An old woman in a grass-stained housedress looking at her like that made Sissy Potash totter again. She glanced down at her bitten knee, and then at Elena, whose hair was standing up like a miniature forest fire. *They're all crazy,* she was probably thinking. What a story!

"It's a charming story, Lulu, and I'm sure your heart's in the right place, but I know something you don't. I'm afraid I have some information that will shock you. Grammie, Mr. and Mrs. Duckworth-Greene—"

"Let me tell them!" Lulu cried. "I already know, Tilda told me, she trusted me!" She hardly recognized her own voice, it was so fierce. "Tilda's a robber! She's a fugitive from justice!"

"Did you say . . . robber?" asked David.

"I'm afraid so, Mr. Duckworth-Greene. She stole money from her mother's bank account. A sizable amount of money. When her mother saw the story about Lulu in the *Plain Dealer,* she contacted me, and I promised her I'd find Tilda. And now, thanks to Lulu, I have."

Sissy Potash picked up her tape recorder and moved toward the door.

"Where do you think you're going? You can't go yet!" Lulu jumped up. Jenny cried louder. Sissy Potash put a hand over her ear.

"I have another appointment. Thanks for your cooperation, Lulu. Don't worry. I don't blame you."

"But we're not finished explaining things to you yet!"

Lulu's father jumped up, then Mrs. Wysocki. They all crowded after the reporter into the hall. Grammie followed with Jenny, whose lung power had reached full capacity.

"You don't understand!" said Lulu. "Things aren't the way they look!"

"Let me tell you about that screen one more time!" said Mrs. Wysocki. "If only I'd known—"

"A journalist's job is to uncover the truth. Nothing more, nothing less. I know you meant well, Lulu. Don't worry, I don't blame you for what you did. But it's plain that Tilda and her baby need more help than a ten-year-old girl is equipped to give." Jenny screamed, and Sissy winced. "This must have been a nightmare for that poor child."

"She's never been happier in her life!" Lulu shouted over the screaming.

Sissy Potash put a hand on the doorknob. "Lulu, I don't think you under—"

"You're not sending her back!" Lulu yelled so loud, she drowned out Jenny. "Tilda made some mistakes! She's had a losing streak. Everybody does sometimes. Didn't you ever?"

"Lulu, I can see you're a very passionate, very strong girl. You're a hero! But you have to understand—"

"In baseball you always get another chance, and you don't give up on your team. That's how it's supposed to be! Tilda's going to find a job any day now. You can't want something as bad as she does and it doesn't come true. Besides, she's got help now. It's not just the two of them anymore. Now it's—"

"Mr. and Mrs. Duckworth-Greene, I'm sure you understand what I'm saying. Could you please explain to Lulu?" She turned the doorknob.

Lulu grabbed her arm. "I'm not letting you go call her mother!"

"Mr. and Mrs. Duckworth-Greene!" Sissy Potash looked down at Lulu's hand, which had her in an iron grip. "Could you please call off your daughter?"

"Lulu Leone, what's the matter with you?" Elena stepped forward. Her red hair stood on end, and her amber eyes glowed like a lion's. "Stop that shouting!"

"No! I'll shout till you all understand! I know you're mad at me! I know you're disappointed again! But Jenny jumped! She wanted to see what life was like out there. And she jumped right to me! Maybe it wasn't an accident. Tilda's my friend. I know how she feels about stuff, and I know she's a really good person. And I'm going to help her, no matter what you all—"

Suddenly her mother yanked her and pinched the back of her neck so hard, Lulu fell speechless with astonishment.

"I don't know what's gotten into her, Ms. Potash. Lulu's usually a very shy kid. All this excitement is making her flip. She's even losing her memory. She must have completely forgotten. Bertie—Tilda—whatever her name is—she *does* have a job."

Sissy Potash's hand froze on the doorknob. Not another surprise from these crazies!

"What?" she said.

"She hasn't started yet, but she has a job. I mean, if

she wants it. I'm not exactly the world's easiest person to work with."

"*You?*"

"That's right. I have my own business. As a matter of fact, I was written up in your paper's magazine section once, when one of my houses won a civic improvement award. I do quality work, Ms. Potash. Just like my mother—I only hang around with quality people."

Sissy Potash blinked rapidly several times, like a fluorescent light about to go on the fritz. Jenny suddenly stopped crying. David took her from Grammie and hoisted her into the air. He rubbed her belly with his shaggy head, and the baby gave a gulp, as if trying to decide whether to laugh or cry.

Lulu knew just how she felt.

"That's right," said Grammie. "If anybody has any questions about Bertie and Datsun, send them to me. That monkey makes me laugh, and Bertie makes the world's best scrambled-egg sandwich. An old lady couldn't ask for better companions."

"If Tilda's mother wants her money back right away, I'm sure Elena could give her an advance on her pay," said David.

Sissy Potash swayed on her purple heels. "I don't understand. I came here to unravel a mystery. Now it seems as if you all knew what was going on all along. Is this some kind of conspiracy?"

"Life's full of surprises," said Elena. She gave the reporter a consoling little pat on the back. "I guess you don't have any children, or you'd know that."

"Didn't you say you had another appointment?" David, still holding Jenny, swung the front door open. "Sorry you have to run. Let us hear from you after you call Tilda's mother."

But now Tilda spoke. "I'll call my mother myself," she said.

"Great," said David. He swung the door wider. "Thanks for stopping in, Ms. Potash," he said, as if she were a customer in his shop.

"Bye-bye, Dodash!" Jenny called happily.

Sissy Potash stepped out and then turned to look at them all crowded there in the doorway. "How did I wind up out here all of a sudden?" her face asked.

"Of course . . . of course I'll contact Tilda's mother immediately! And I'll be following up on this story closely."

She rubbed her bitten knee, whirled around, nearly fell over Jenny's stroller, and wobbled down the front walk.

Chapter 25

As the red car pulled away, Mrs. Wysocki wiped her forehead with a meaty arm.

"Phew!" she said. "That woman gives me the heebie-jeebies!"

"You're not the only one," said Elena.

Mrs. Wysocki turned to Tilda. "I should've noticed that screen myself, but I didn't. As nosy as I am, as God is my witness. But if you would've just told me—"

"You're right," said Tilda quietly. "It's not your fault. Stop worrying about it."

"When it's fixed, that's when I stop worrying about it." Mrs. Wysocki clamped a hand on Lulu's shoulder. "I get the feeling we're not going to be on *Stars of the Heights,* dearie. That's a shame, because you're a good girl. God in heaven! My head feels like it went through a meat grinder." She slipped her rhinestone sunglasses back on.

"Can I give you a ride someplace?" David asked her.

"Walking will steady my nerves."

But on the front steps she turned. "It looks like you found yourself a good situation," she said to Tilda. "Not your everyday situation, but good. You probably won't believe me, but I'm glad for you and the baby. Let me know when you're ready to come get your crib."

"Bye-bye!" said Jenny. Then she yelled, "Datsun!" and reached for Lulu.

"She sure does like you," David said, handing his daughter the baby. "But how come she calls you Datsun?"

"We don't know. It's like she thinks I have another identity or something."

"Honey," said Lulu's father, "you just proved to us all that you do."

Lulu bent her head and pretended to wipe crumbs from Jenny's lips. If there was one thing a baby was good for, it was an excuse not to meet other people's eyes.

Tilda made that gargling noise. Lulu knew she was overwhelmed by how everyone had stood up for her. She'd come here expecting to fight off enemies—and instead she had found herself in the center of a family. Not your everyday family, that was for sure. But then, would someone like her have fit into a normal family, if there was such a thing? At last she spoke.

"I'm sorry I wrecked Lulu's interview. Mrs. Wysocki's right. She's never going to be on TV now."

There was a pause, and then Elena said quietly, "Then TV's missing the biggest story of all."

Lulu looked up into her mother's eyes.

"You were right, lambchop," Elena said. "Catching Jenny was a far-out thing to do, but it didn't make you a hero. Catching her was like—like having a baby! Glory! Ecstasy! The Hallelujah Chorus! But taking care of the baby afterward—now, that's the hard part."

"Catching a ball's a pleasure, but knowing what to do with it's business." Tilda blushed. "I read that in *Baseball Digest,*" she blurted.

Grammie, Elena, and David all laughed.

"Right!" said Elena. "Exactly!"

"Zacley!" said Jenny.

"Did you really mean that, Mrs. Duckworth-Greene? About—you know. Giving me a job? You don't even know me."

David smiled at Tilda. "We know how much you mean to Lulu. I guess that's enough of a character reference."

"Don't know *you,*" said Elena. "I guess that's not all I don't know." Elena touched Lulu's baseball cap, still perched on Jenny's head. "Last night when I told you I felt like we were strangers—I was right, wasn't I, lambchop? All these years I've pushed you—didn't I have eyes in my head? Did I need glasses?"

"You're right about one thing, Mrs. Duckworth-Greene," said Tilda. "Lulu's a lot braver than she thinks she is. Every time I was ready to give up, she convinced me not to. I—you know. Gave her a pretty hard time. But she wouldn't quit on me. Once she set her mind to help me, she would've gone through fire for me."

"And you did it all yourself," said Elena softly. "All this time, you never asked for help."

Lulu looked at her mother. "Maybe I should've."

"Not you," said Grammie. "You're too stubborn. You're just as much of a mule as your mother."

Elena's laugh was gentle and sad. "You mean we do have something in common after all?"

Then, somehow, Lulu and her mother were in each other's arms. The small hard thing inside Lulu began to swell, and then it burst, like a flower opening in a speeded-up film.

Chapter 26

That very afternoon, Tilda and Jenny took the bus home.

"I can't just call my mother up," Tilda said. "I have to go see her and—you know. Talk to her."

Elena drove them to the bus station. Just before they boarded their bus, she gave Tilda a check.

Tilda looked at it as if it were a lighted firecracker. Then she hugged Jenny to her and took the bus steps two at a time.

Two days went by. David went to Mrs. Wysocki's and got the crib and a few other things Tilda and Lulu hadn't been able to carry. The screen, he said, had been replaced.

The Indians beat the Yankees with a ninth-inning, bases-loaded double by Bert Watson and moved up to next-to-last place.

Lulu played a game. Her first at-bat, she struck out. Her second, she went 3 and 2, then blooped a double to center.

It was her first hit of the season. The lawn chairs went wild. She was sure she could hear her mother yelling louder than anyone. As she rounded first and saw the fielders still scrambling and the coach beckoning, all she could think was, *Tilda! You taught me to do this!*

That night, as she and her parents were finishing supper (chicken with mushrooms and wine for them, plain for Lulu), the phone rang. Tilda was back at Grammie's.

"Can you come over? I need to—you know."

"Talk."

"Yeah."

"I'll be right there."

When Lulu rode up, Tilda was sitting on the front steps. A glove Lulu didn't recognize dangled from one hand.

"It's mine from home. Grammie took Jenny for ice cream. She said you and I should go have a catch."

They practiced for a long time before Tilda walked over to the sidelines and sat down. Lulu followed her.

"What was it like?"

"Pretty bad. Jenny whined the whole time. I think she really missed you and Grammie."

"Did your mom say she was going to press charges or anything?"

"At first she called me a lot of names. Jenny tried to bite her, but I caught her in time. When I gave her your mother's check, she said I probably just forged it. I told her she had her right to say that, considering, but I wasn't going to do things like that anymore. I said I met some people that—you know. Were giving me a chance.

"It was really weird. She wanted to know all about you and your parents and Grammie. When she finally got it through her head that I was coming back here, she just about started crying!"

Tilda looked out over the mound. She pressed her lips together hard.

"She wanted to know why I wasn't happy at home, and didn't I believe she always tried to do the best she could for me. Sissy Potash called a couple of times, and my mother told her to mind her own business! Butt out! She started trying to convince me to—you know. Give living there one more chance."

Tilda dug her toe in the dirt. Lulu saw she'd gotten new laces for her hightops.

"But I said no. It made me feel so bad to see her cry. But it made me want to kill her too! Why'd she have to wait till I was leaving to say she wanted me?"

Lulu looked at the little rut Tilda's toe had made.

"I'm sure glad you came back," she said. "But maybe

you could visit your mom sometimes. Or talk on the phone. Or write letters. Maybe you could get to know each other better."

Tilda squinted into the setting sun. "Maybe," she said. "Maybe."

They sat there a little longer, and then Tilda said she'd better get back. She was starting work for Elena tomorrow morning, and she wanted to get a good night's sleep.

As they rode home, Lulu told Tilda she'd hit a double that day.

"I did what you said. I loosened up. I took it easy. I wasn't scared."

"I was wondering, riding home on the bus. Do you think Coach Angell could use any more volunteers?"

"You mean *you*?"

Tilda smiled. "No, that dog peeing on the fence. You know what Grammie was telling me tonight? That restaurant where she and her friends go out to lunch sponsors a women's softball team. I wonder if they have any rules against somebody joining this late in the season."

"Once they see you pitch, they'll smash any rule they have to smithereens."

They were at Grammie's house. "Wait a minute," said Tilda. "I brought you something back."

She ran inside and came back out with a baseball cap.

"It was mine," she said, "when I was in Little League."

"Really? You wore this?"

Lulu pulled it on. The visor slanted down to her nose. "Now I know how Jenny feels inside my cap," she said.

Tilda laughed. "You'll grow into it."

"It's probably the best present anybody ever gave me."

Lulu wore the cap backward as she rode home. Though she had avoided it ever since that fateful day, tonight she rode past Mrs. Wysocki's apartment building. She stopped her bike for a moment and looked up at it. She tried to remember when the place hadn't meant anything to her. For at least a year she'd ridden past it and hardly even noticed it. Then, in that one instant she'd looked up, nearly everything had changed.

As she rode on, Lulu had a funny feeling that other surprises might be lurking where she'd never expected them. Who knew who lived behind those windows with the jungle-print curtains? Who knew what might happen if she went up to that girl with the sticking-out braids and told her, "I've seen you about a million times, sitting on your front steps with your chin in your hands—what are you dreaming about, anyway?" Who knew what kind of surprises might be camouflaged in people and places she thought she already knew?

The thought made her feel suddenly rich. When she got to the hill just beyond Dairy Dell, she let go of the handlebars and coasted the whole way no-handed. She didn't hit one rock or pothole.

At home, her father had the Indians game on. Lulu sprawled on the floor beside him.

"Is Tilda okay?"

"I think so."

"Bases are loaded and the count's three and two. Carter's had three foul tips in a row."

"And the pitch . . . ," said the announcer, just as Elena walked into the room.

Carter slammed it. That ball didn't have a chance. David pulled Lulu's cap off and tossed it into the air.

"A grand slam! How do you like that—a grand slam!"

"What's a grand slam?" asked Elena.

She put her head on the floor and slowly unfolded herself in a yoga headstand, as Lulu carefully, patiently explained.

About the Author

TRICIA SPRINGSTUBB is the author of numerous short stories, picture books, and young adult novels, including *Give and Take* and *The Moon on a String.* She is the author of a trilogy of books detailing the adventures of Eunice Gottlieb: *Which Way to the Nearest Wilderness?, Eunice Gottlieb and the Unwhitewashed Truth about Life,* and *Eunice (the Egg Salad) Gottlieb,* as well as *With a Name Like Lulu, Who Needs More Trouble?*

Tricia Springstubb lives in Cleveland Heights, Ohio, with her husband and three children, Zoe, Phoebe, and Delia.